THE SONG
of the Locust

Published 2012 by Teramar Media, Inc.

West Palm Beach, FL USA

ISBN: 0615704883

ISBN-13: 9780615704883

THE SONG
of the Locust

A NOVEL

BARBARA JULIETTE KLINGER

With love to my grandchildren
Rachel and Alexander

Acknowledgements

The source of my inspiration as a writer has always ensued from the
relationships with the special people in my life.

My heartfelt thanks go to my love and Life Partner, Philippe Brian,
for his unquestioned support of my efforts.

Special thanks to my precious daughters Alexandra and Lisa and my
granddaughter Stephanie and my grandson David, for
their unwavering belief in me.

Most of all, my deepest thanks go to my dearest friend and editor,
Margarita Pardo Abrishami, whose work I truly value
and whose wisdom is priceless.

Chapter one

May twelfth was the most important day of the year for Antonio–his birthday. Even more important, it was Rachel's birthday, too. From the time they were small children, Antonio and Rachel had celebrated their birthdays together. These days they were forced to live apart. Now, as he kept running, his breath getting shorter and heavier by the minute, Antonio was determined to make this year no different than the others: Even if it meant putting himself in danger.

Just an hour ago, his spiky black hair was fresh and clean. At this moment, every strand clung to his head, heavy beads of perspiration weighing them down. A sharp pain thrust through his chest. He stopped for a moment, bent forward, and took a few deep breaths.

Antonio was tall, slender and thirteen years old, and he was scared. "OMG, I'm getting sick!" He spoke his frustration aloud, even though no one was around to hear. He was mad at himself for being afraid, but as he gasped for breath, he gritted his teeth determined to continue his journey. "What's wrong with me? I've never felt this way before."

Beads of perspiration gathered on his forehead and dripped into his eyes, burning them. Had he overestimated his own strength?

For a moment, he stood still, looking around. Again, he spoke aloud. "Please help me; I'm so confused!" He was no longer sure of what to do. Suddenly, a whispered thought gently entered his mind.

> *Run. Run. Remember if you do not get there before your parents read the note, your plan will be over before it begins.*

He stumbled forward, at first only a few feet at a time, and then began gaining strength and running again. His thoughts were running as fast as his feet. "Okay. I feel much better now that I'm gaining speed again. I know it'll be alright!" He thought about where he was headed, and his young body gained even more strength. He was now ready to do the most daring thing he'd ever done in his life!

"Deep breaths; keep running," he told himself. "In a few minutes you'll be on that wall. You're very close to it even now." He kept running and taking deep breaths, thoughts of Rachel fueling his progress. "Our parents just don't understand that we have feelings just like they do. We're very young but we love each other so much, and we'll be best friends forever. I want to go to school with Rachel again, do homework together! When we grow up, we'll get married just like other people in love." The thought brought a sweet smile to his tired face.

It was already the sixth of May, but if everything went well he'd be on time for her birthday, and his. They'd always thought how special it was to have their birthdays on the same day. He had one week to get there and then they could have their birthday party; only this time, it would be at her new home in America.

Excitement stirred him and his eyes sparkled like amber lights in a golden fire. Once again he resolved, "I *will* get there; I'm sure of it. My plan *has* to work!" He glanced back for the last time at the green hills and familiar places of home, his eyes blurring as he gazed all the way to the horizon. As if he had never seen it before, he stood there, amazed at the beauty of the sunset. He shook his head. He had to keep moving. He had to keep going in spite of the odds, just to keep his dream alive.

No hesitation now: Antonio sped up, his baggy jeans and the blue sweatshirt wrapped around his waist slowing him down. He wished he'd worn something more practical, but what? He had worn what he typically wore, the oversized T-shirt clinging to his body even as sweat trickled down his back. He had put on blue sneakers without socks, and the constant rubbing from the run was beginning to hurt.

The tall gray wall finally appeared in front of him. He often went there with his soccer buddy Mario, just curious to see if anything unusual was happening. Yet every time they came to the border, he was amazed at what a peaceful place it actually was.

He looked around. Empty. Quiet. He could hear only the smooth buzzing of big black flies and the sporadic chirping of tiny black birds. Their noise was the only sound that filled the surrounding area as they flew above the tall green trees. He could almost feel the emptiness. Awesome; no one else was there. He allowed himself a brief moment of celebration.

Then he sped up as much as he could, lifting up with lean athletic arms, pushing fully off the ground, fingers clenching on to the very edge of the wall. He swung his long legs up, and quickly found himself flat on his belly and looking down at the other side.

Antonio lay there motionless with his eyes wide open, listening to every sound around him. He could hear only the singing birds and buzzing insects flying above. He had made it! It looked like everything would be okay after all!

Antonio's eyes darted in every direction to make sure nothing escaped his attention. The quiet around him and the soft whisper in his ear told him it was safe to move. Wait. Whisper in his ear? What was this about? Even as he heard the gentle whisper, he couldn't believe what he heard. Maybe he was going crazy; it happened to people all the time. However, he had no time to pay attention to his doubts, no time to think.

As slow as an inchworm, he crawled over to the other side of the wall and again became motionless as he looked around warily. "OMG I'm in America!" he whispered. "*Adios* Mexico, I love you but I love Rachel more. I promise to visit you when I'm older."

He closed his eyes and waited until his heart beat slower. This was the most daring thing he'd ever done. Antonio really tried to think it through, but couldn't absorb the thought. He only sat there, amazed at his own actions. Slowly his body relaxed and he inhaled deeply.

It was just as he had planned! In a few days he would see his friend Rachel again. For a brief moment Antonio was so proud and happy he almost began to sing the American anthem! He stopped himself just in time: Even a small noise could alert the border patrol. He quickly sobered up. He wondered if he would be in more trouble with his parents or with the border patrol!

Now feeling safe and free, he rolled himself to the very edge of the wall on the American side and dropped down: Soon he would run on American soil. He felt like screaming loudly so he could be heard all the way to Rachel's new home: "I'm on my way; I'll see you soon!"

The ginger edge of the sun touched the horizon and he admired the changing colors of the sky and the landscape. Somehow he understood that he would never see his surroundings the same way again. He stared at the tall green trees and clumpy bushes illuminated by the orange, red and golden hues. Even as he paused to look, the sun continued its rapid descent to the ends of the earth and he stood there, mesmerized. He didn't want to miss one detail of this experience. He just knew that someday he would share the story of this journey with his schoolmates and family, and he cherished the moment.

Instantly the sky became dark orange, then dark red and a heavy veil of white and gray clouds swallowed the glow of the day. He had the strangest sensation of the world around him coming to a complete stop.

Antonio swallowed hard. Suddenly he felt very much his age and overwhelmed by loneliness. He began to miss his home and family, the comfort of his room, and his things—his guitar and books, his sports trophies. He even missed school! He felt a weird sensation, as if the sky were closing in on him and his recent happy thoughts evaporated as quickly as the setting sun. He had an unmistakable urge to jump back over the wall and run all the way home.

What had he done? He had broken the rules, that's what! What would happen if he were caught by the border guards? Guilt overcame him, numbing his senses. Again he spoke aloud, almost like a prayer: "I don't know what to do, please help me."

The strange whisper teased him.

Think of Rachel. She is the reason you are here.

There it was again! He pinched his earlobe very hard, trying to understand the source of the soothing whisper. What was that? OMG, was he losing his mind?

Urgently, more than a little frightened, he slipped his hand into his upper pocket searching for his iPhone. It was gone! Only a few protein bars and small tubes of energy drinks were there.

Antonio trembled and his hands began to shake. He felt like he was freaking out; he gasped for air. "I'm so stupid, leaving it in my pocket." He wanted to scream in frustration. He checked again in both pockets, but the iPhone was truly gone! He had planned to use it as the link to where he came from and where he was going. Now what? He was terribly frightened. But the whisper in his ear didn't give up.

> *You know the purpose of being here. Calm down: You*
> *will be fine, you will survive; this is no time to give up.*

"Okay I *will* relax and get a hold of myself." He started to meditate as his *Abuelita* Hope had taught him, to empty his mind completely. "I'm free." He repeated it over and over, until the silence in the darkness was interrupted by the whirring and steady sound of a solitary locust.

To his ear, it sounded like the prolonged pressing of the highest note of the piano key, followed by a short pause. Again playing louder and softer, and on, and off, and on again.

He'd never paid much attention to the outdoor sounds of the evening. Now he had all the time in the world to do just that. He instantly relaxed and was rewarded with the soft embrace of the darkened world around him. It was time to go to sleep, but Antonio was still leaning on the American side of the wall, planning his escape. His thoughts raced on. "I know I'll have many difficult days ahead, but there's no way I'm going back home. My mind is made up. No matter what, I'm going to America: I'm going home to Rachel."

He let out a soft sigh and lay down, stretching his entire body and making sure he was completely covered by the surrounding thick bushes. Still trying to clear his mind and to rid himself of guilt, he focused on the gray sky covered with scattered white clouds and the shining stars between them. Then he did what came the most naturally: He recited the prayer to his guardian angel, as he did every night before going to sleep.

The singing of the lone locust became softer as it stopped and began again, going on and off. Now it sounded like the twanging of a solitary guitar just like the one Antonio had left at home. His heart ached again. No matter how he tried not to feel guilty he couldn't stop the feelings. Most of all he was sorry for the pain he knew he was giving his parents and Rachel.

"I'm sure they're all worrying about me, but it's done, and I can't change it now. I really didn't plan to lose my iPhone! Anyway, if I hadn't run away, I probably would never see Rachel again." He knew he had made the right decision to cross the border. But at what cost to everybody? He consoled himself. "By now my parents are reading my note; they know I'm on my way to America. Only, they'll want to stop me. For sure they've notified the border control and soon they'll search for me. There's no way I'll let them get me!" He smiled with a mischievous twinkle in his amber eyes.

Maybe he should just keep going right now. He lifted his head and looked around. Everything was calm and there was nothing to be afraid of. He realized that his feelings had gone from nervous to relaxed and back again in just a few moments. He was almost ready to get going again, and then, the strange whisper came to soothe him.

You know, if you start to run, your plans will be over;
it is better if you stay put, for now. You are well hidden.

"Wow! Am I dreaming? These strange whispers are beginning to frighten me." He tried to see in the darkness, something, *anything,* but it was useless. "Is anybody out there?"

Maybe he was imagining the whole thing; maybe there was something wrong with him! Yet, there was a soothing familiarity to the sounds. He hesitated only briefly, and finally decided to listen to that voice. He lay his head back against the wall and lingered there, hiding behind the thick bushes and leaves of the closest tree. Not moving one finger, he just listened to every sound.

"I don't hear anything, but I'll wait until midnight. I bet that'll be the best way to stay safe."

The locust's song was getting softer, and it almost hypnotized him. "If I think of Rachel I won't feel alone, and maybe I'll even fall asleep." He closed his eyes, thinking of Rachel and planning his trip.

"I'll be okay; I won't get lost. I looked the maps up on Google and I paid attention to all those National Geographic programs my dad made me watch on TV. I just need to find the S-2 Highway and run near it; that will be the easiest and fastest way to get to Laguna Beach."

He took a deep breath and smiled to himself. "Anyway, I have a GPS right in my head! Why shouldn't I make it? So many others get across the border without half of my preparations! I *will* make it; I know I will!"

He reached into his pocket, pulled out a protein bar and an energy drink and, as he was eating, he heard the locust again. "What if I could become a locust for my trip?" he mused. "It would be so great: I could fly just like they do. I would be so small that no one would find me. And they are free; they sound truly happy. It would be easy to get to America as a tiny insect!" Even as he thought about it, Antonio started to feel really strange. His world was changing, and he didn't even realize it. "Forget about being able to fly," he told himself. "You're no Harry Potter!" He laughed. It was really time to sleep if he was thinking about magic spells!

After he swallowed the last bite of food, a gentle breeze of sweet perfume caressed his face. His nose twitched and he covered it quickly with his hand to prevent a loud sneeze. For a while he took many deep breaths and finally began to feel relaxed. He yawned a few times and, as that soothing puff of sweet fragrance caressed his face again, all discomfort was suddenly gone. The guilty feelings evaporated, his fears subsided and he felt more positive and calm than he had since he began his journey.

A soft laugh vibrated in the air, and again the sweet perfume brushed his face. This time the fragrance was very strong, but being so tired, he just accepted what his senses were telling him and he thought about his upcoming trip. Still sleepless, he started to think about every feature of the desert: The dry and desolate hills, the scattered ponds, the cactuses, the fruit bushes, the little creatures and the predators. He even remembered the forgotten ghost towns! He again fantasized about how cool it would be to become as tiny as a locust, if just for the night.

As his jumbled thoughts tumbled through his tired mind, he could hear the whisper in his ear again.

Relax!

This time the tone was more firm, but still sweet.

You just rest; tomorrow is another day. Mañana será otro día.

Where had he heard that expression before? He couldn't remember. He felt the fragrant breeze brushing his face; he became drowsy, his lids heavy. In a split second he was asleep, and he never even heard the border patrol as they looked for him.

Chapter two

Antonio and his parents lived in Mexico, in the little town of Cocobana inhabited by just about ten thousand people. It was located a few miles from the Southern California border.

His father, Paulo Molino, a forty-six year old dentist, had been educated in Mexico City. Tall, golden-skinned and slender, he was as friendly as he was competent. All the people in town respected Paulo. His eyes, charcoal orbs sprinkled with silver dust, were set strong in an oval face that shone with kindness. His wife liked to tease him: With his hair brushed straight back, trimmed to perfection, he had the look of a professional tango dancer! Appearances aside, he loved his medical calling, and gave his best care to every person who needed his help at any time.

Antonio's mother Sara was thirty-six years old. A petite woman, she still looked like a college student with her tortoise shell eyeglasses, her hair long and black, swinging side to side over her shoulders. An olive complexion and full mouth gave her a very exotic look. Her love of walking kept her young and slim. "I love to see the town when I walk," she would often say to her family. "That's why I walk to work. It gives me the best exercise and lets me think and relax at the same time." This love of exercise had rubbed off on her son, Antonio.

Sara was the town's librarian and all the inhabitants of Cocobana knew her for her gentle nature. She was always helpful to both young and old in finding books and answering questions, her large eyes sparkling like black diamonds when she was challenged by an especially difficult topic.

The Molinos lived in a six room, two story stucco and brick home with a red clay roof and a small but beautiful fenced garden full of colorful hibiscus and white roses. Antonio was their only child and Rachel was his best friend and neighbor.

Rachel's family, the Olsenos, had been the Molinos' closest neighbors since the children were babies. The Olsenos were both doctors and they had two children, Rachel and her younger brother, ten year old Alexander. Roberto and Juliette Olseno had met while studying at the Philadelphia Jefferson University Medical School. They had fallen in love at first sight and were still considered the perfect couple by everybody, especially themselves!

Roberto Olseno was born in Mexico and his wife, Juliette, was born in America. Now they were inseparable, even sharing an office. Both were tall and slender. Both had almond shaped faces and thick sun-kissed brown hair speckled with strands of blond. Juliette wore her long hair pinned in a bun on the side, showing off her pretty profile and perky nose to perfection. Roberto wore his hair cut with a slight spike near his forehead, giving him a very modern look. When the couple smiled, revealing their perfect white teeth, they looked just like a pair of teens! The Olsenos received much attention from strangers wherever they went, something that, of course, embarrassed their children greatly!

For a long time the couple had been thinking of moving to America, specifically Laguna Beach in California. Juliette's mom Bobbi, the Olseno children's grandma, had moved there from Philadelphia when she became widowed. She liked the climate and natural beauty, and was happy being closer to her family in Mexico. A typical grandmother, she was hoping that someday her children and grandchildren would leave Mexico and live near her. This was also the dream of Rachel's mom, Juliette.

Rachel and Antonio were very close friends and neighbors. They went to the same private school where they learned both Spanish and English. Their parents became very close friends, having dinner at each other's homes and always available to baby-sit for each other.

Antonio's parents also wanted to move to America, but for them it was mostly a dream. They were aware of the difficulties involved in immigrating to America, but it was more than that. The real problem was that the Molinos felt genuinely needed by the folks in Cocobana. They were well educated, professional Mexicans, and understood their talents were an asset to their community. Everybody in town knew what good and loyal members of the community the Molinos were.

As very caring citizens who loved both their country and their hometown, they hesitated to leave. So this is how Antonio came to believe that his parents would never move to America.

Chapter three

It was a very bright June morning as Rachel, dressed in her navy blue school uniform, brushed her long sun-kissed brown hair and stood in front of the hallway mirror, wondering about her future. She looked at her reflection, thinking how she looked just like her mother. This was a good thing, but she didn't quite appreciate it yet. She was nearly thirteen but tall for her age, standing at almost six feet. The perky nose, thick hair, full lips and long legs were all there, but she had yet to grow into her features. She sighed. "Well, I may be tall but at least I'm a good basketball player!" The fact that she also played softball, edited the school newspaper and loved art, made her an all around favorite at her school.

She sighed again. With wonderful caring parents, and a "not so bad" younger brother, she was usually happy. But not today. This morning, as she looked at herself in the mirror, she didn't like what she saw. Her eyes didn't sparkle like diamonds, and the smile didn't glow on her face. "How can I be happy," she thought, "if I have to tell Antonio my really bad news today?" Rachel had been dreading this moment for a long time. She took a deep breath, grabbed her backpack, and hugged her mom. Suddenly, she was in a rush to go.

As usual, Antonio was waiting for her in front of his house. Holding his books he smiled and walked towards her. He quickly bent his tall slender body, took the books from Rachel, and then had good look at her.

"Hey Rachel, what's wrong? Did you have a fight with your parents or something?" Rachel glanced at his happy face. "I will miss him so much," she thought. As always his clean black hair shone with health and his amber eyes sparkled with interest as he looked back at her. "He is so kind to me—to everybody. He is so fun to be with. How can I ruin his day with my news?" So instead of telling him her problems she just said, "Antonio, you look great today!" In the navy blue uniform, white shirt and tie, and the eternal smile on his face, he *did* look so handsome. "So do you Rachel," he replied. However, he was still worried about her. He knew all of her moods and something was going on.

All of a sudden, Rachel burst into tears. Antonio stopped walking and gently grabbed her arm. He asked again, "What's bothering you, why can't you tell me? You used to tell me everything."

Tears were rolling down her face. "Antonio, we are leaving for America as soon as the school year is over! My parents have already rented a house in Irvine, in California, near to Laguna Beach where my grandma lives. It's a very beautiful place, but I'm so unhappy!"

Now she was sobbing and he didn't know how to comfort her. "My mom wants to live near my grandmother. She's already enrolled us in the Plaza Vista School." Her voice was shaking. "Mom says it's a very good school," Rachel added as an afterthought.

Antonio dropped their books to the ground and awkwardly put his arms around his best friend. Now he had tears in his eyes, too. "I never really thought this would ever happen."

"I didn't either," she answered, swallowing her tears. Rachel wiped her eyes with the back of her hand and let go of Antonio's gentle hug.

"We have to go, you know. Or we will be late for algebra class." He agreed, thinking how his friend was always practical. Silently, side by side, they continued to walk to school.

Antonio was a gentle teenager, but suddenly he exploded with anger: "Grownups really don't care how we feel, but I promise you and I promise myself, no matter where and how, we will be together again!" He kicked a small stone laying in front of him with such force that it flew far away, and got lost in the bushes of somebody's garden.

Rachel looked at him, smiling again. She had complete trust in her best friend, Antonio.

Chapter four

A year had passed since Rachel had moved away and nothing was ever the same again. Antonio missed Rachel more each day and even his grades were falling. His teacher became concerned and called his mother, Sara, for a conference.

"I think he's just not studying and I don't understand why," the teacher said to Sara when they met after school. Sara knew exactly what was bothering Antonio. "Let me talk to him," she replied. "I promise I will work with him and he will pick up his grades again." But Sara knew in her heart that it was not a matter of just working with Antonio. She sighed and prepared to talk to him when she got home.

After returning to the house, Sara walked up to Antonio's room and found him sitting on the bed playing his guitar. She sat down next to him, and gently asked, "Antonio, what is happening? Your grades have fallen and your teacher is worried." He shrugged his shoulders, assuming an uncharacteristically calm and stoic manner.

"I miss Rachel. Does that surprise you?" he grumbled in an irritated voice. Sara looked at him, her soulful eyes showing a mom's understanding.

She took his face into her hands and looked into his now always sad eyes. It hurt her so much to see him this way!

"Antonio, *querido,* please be realistic. We will visit her soon, I promise. You must be reasonable and understand that we just can't move to America right now. Your *papa* has to be ready to leave his practice here and be able to work there as a dentist. It takes so much time!"

"I don't want to visit! I want to live near Rachel! You don't understand; you just don't understand!" Antonio had actually raised his voice at his mother, something he had never done before.

Sara tried not to feel hurt. She knew that dealing with teenage outbursts was part of being a mom. She reasoned with him again. *"Mi'jo,* we bought you an iPhone so that you could constantly be in contact with your friend. You can call, text, send emails, even pictures. We never limit your time." Antonio just rolled his eyes and began to play his guitar again. The tune was *"La Paloma"*, a song that Rachel liked best. Rachel even used to sing it with him.

Sara comforted herself as he strummed the soulful tune. "Well, I've done my best for now. He'll be alright; these teenage problems never end." She kissed him on the forehead.

"When your father comes home we'll talk about it some more." Her dark eyes filled with tears. It was tough to see her son hurt so much. "I wish Paulo were home already. I need him to be here, to help me with Antonio. A son always listens to his *papa."*

She walked to the white sofa in the living room and tried to get comfortable to wait for her husband. Sara remembered how as a young girl herself, her *mama,* Antonio's grandmother, had taught her to meditate. She quieted her thoughts and began to take deep breaths, her green dress gently moving to the rhythm of her breaths. However, nothing could take away her anxiety! Her only son was unhappy and she just did not know how to fix it.

Finally, she heard the door open. It was six o'clock and time for dinner. Sara could not even *think* of food, let alone cooking. Every time she got upset, she lost her appetite and didn't want to be *near* the kitchen! Paulo came in expecting dinner, but one look at his wife told him "the kitchen was closed", as he liked to say. Sara's unhappy face showed him why.

"What's wrong, *querida?*" He quickly got an earful from a very upset Sara. "Refreshments are in order," he thought as he bent down to embrace her. Paulo kissed her cheek and said, "How about if I get us both a glass of nice, cold iced tea? We'll both feel better with something cool to drink. I'll be right back." He proceeded to remove his white work jacket and walked to the refrigerator at the bar. Filling two tall glasses with iced tea, he made his way back to his wife.

"Now, tell me what's really going on, Sara." He handed his wife a glass and took a sip of his own. "Did you have a bad day at the library?" She glanced at him with tearful eyes, and began to tell him about Antonio. They could both hear the guitar as Antonio played alone upstairs.

Paulo listened to every word with undivided attention. When she finished, he wrapped his arm around her shoulder and comforted her.

"I will go up and talk to him. He's old enough to understand that we can't just leave our country without thought or planning." He glanced out the window saying, "I would like to live in America, maybe someday, but not now. It's just impossible for us to do that now."

His voice was somber. When he finished sipping the drink, he climbed the stairs, knocked at Antonio's door, pushed it gently and walked in. Antonio was sitting on the twin bed covered with a sky blue comforter, hugging his guitar. He stared out the window overlooking the house where Rachel used to live.

Paulo sat down next to him and put his arm around his son, saying, "How are you *mi'jo?* I hear you're having a problem with your grades. You miss soccer practice and you don't want to see your friends after school. What is going on in that wonderful head of yours?"

Affectionately he placed his finger under Antonio's chin and lifted it up to wait for his son to talk.

"I just don't want to live here since Rachel went away, *Papa.* I want to live near her. Remember how we did homework together, how we rode our bikes and played basketball, how we sang and played the guitar? And now look at my life..."

He paused, swallowing hard. "It's no fun in school anymore. Rachel's old friends Gina and Ana were hitting each other and pulling their hair today. Since Rachel left, now they each want to sit next to me and be my BFF. It's really embarrassing!"

"The guys are making fun of me, teasing me that Rachel didn't care for me and that's why she left. I even got into a fistfight with them after school. Everything is falling apart for me." He swallowed again and stopped talking.

Paulo took a deep breath. He felt sad for his son and couldn't even imagine how bad it was for him. Teasing can easily turn into bullying and he did not want his son to be hurt. Gently he placed his hand on Antonio's shoulder, looked intensely into his eyes and said, "Son, I will take care of the things that are happening in school, I promise you. About being Rachel's neighbors again, well, that will have to wait. We will join them as soon as it is possible. Remember we don't have family in America, and it takes a long time to get the permission to immigrate. Eventually we will get there. But I need you to be patient."

Paulo cleared his throat; he knew that Antonio wasn't going to like what he was about to say. "In the meantime, son, I know you are depressed. I want you to see a friend of mine who is a doctor. I know that it will be very helpful, much more helpful than talking to me."

Antonio shook his head. "No, I don't need to talk to a psychiatrist." Paulo decided to let the protest pass.

"*Mi'jo,* let me see what we have for dinner. When the food is ready I'll call you downstairs and we will talk some more. It's not as tragic as you think; you talk to Rachel every day, and it is only a year since she left, so be patient." He embraced Antonio and walked out.

Antonio strummed his guitar again. After this talk with his parents, he was even more convinced that they just did *not* understand.

Chapter five

In the morning everything went back to normal: Antonio set out for school alone and in a bad mood; his father took off in his sports car to the office; and his mom briskly walked to the library.

Sara had a busy day and was glad when it was finally over. She stopped at the small grocery store near the house and picked up salad greens, tomatoes, hot baked bread and fresh shrimp to make shrimp scampi. She wanted to make a nice dinner for her family since she had not cooked the night before. She sang softly as she walked home; this was Antonio and Paulo's favorite meal and she knew they would have a lovely dinner.

The air was cool and fragrant, a nice change from the previous week. Birds chirped in the trees that lined the quiet streets. During her walk she glanced at the fashionable storefronts while she made plans to take Antonio to the museum the following day. Since it would be a Saturday, she would take him and his friend Mario to their favorite restaurant, Boca.

It was half past four when she arrived home. She glanced fondly at the small fenced garden full of hibiscus, white roses and jasmine just beginning to bloom.

Sara reflected on Antonio's wish to immigrate to America. "How could I ever leave this place? I love it so much here; this is home. Paulo and I have made our life here and this is where Antonio was born. We are respected and liked by the town and Paulo has a thriving dental practice. I love my job and I love my country." A few tears came to her eyes. They would have to work things out as a family.

Distracted, she tried the door, expecting it to open. It was strange. Antonio always left the door open, but today it was locked. She figured he had stopped at Mario's on the way home. Or maybe he had finally remembered to lock the door! She called out to him just to make sure.

"Antonio, I'm home. How was your day?" There was no answer. She put the groceries on the counter and walked upstairs. She knocked on his door. Still no answer and she noticed his bed was neatly made. Then she Saw it—a note placed on the large blue pillow. Sara tried not to panic as she sat down on the bed to read the note. She picked it up with her trembling hands, took a deep breath and began to read.

"*Queridos Mama y Papa*: I'm really sorry to do this to you, but I am on my way to see Rachel. I don't need a psychiatrist and I'm not being a difficult teenager: I just want to see Rachel in America. I love you very much and I will call you when I cross the border and later during my trip."

At first Sara just could not believe what she was reading. Her son went to America by himself? When it finally sunk in, she quickly dialed Antonio's cell. It rang and rang but there was no answer.

Now she dialed her husband's office number. "Paulo, you are not going to believe this! Antonio has left for America; listen to the note he left behind." She read it through her tears.

Paulo reacted quickly. "How could we have misunderstood our son so badly, Sara! Let me hang up and dial for help." Not knowing whom to call, he dialed 911 and asked for the border patrol and the local police. Sara was left alone to worry. Paulo acted on instinct and, dropping everything at the office in the lap of his assistants, he drove to the closest point of the border.

The American side of the border patrol had already been notified by the time Paulo arrived. He and the authorities from both sides searched for hours even after darkness fell, but there was just no sign of Antonio.

Paulo felt shaken and defeated. He hung his head sadly as he finally decided to go home. Then suddenly he noticed something shiny laying on the edge of the border wall: It was Antonio's iPhone! He reached for it and quickly called the search parties. The men waited as he listened to all the messages, hoping for a clue to the boy's location. There were many messages, but only one was important; it was from Rachel. What Paulo heard made him worry even more.

"Don't do anything stupid," said Rachel's voice. "Listen to your parents and me. Eventually we'll be neighbors again and we'll have a wonderful time together. I miss you too, but stay put till your family has handled all the details of moving. I know from my parents that it takes a long time to get the permission to immigrate to America. I love you Antonio. I don't want anything bad to happen to you. I'll talk to you soon. Please be safe."

Paulo's heart was pounding. He blamed himself: "I am not a good father; I didn't communicate well with my son and that is why he left us. I should have done a better job at understanding the situation with Rachel. Perhaps now I have lost my only son to the dangers of the desert." Tears welled in his eyes and he just could not control them.

Sadly, he turned to the border patrol officers. "He is gone. Do you think there is any hope of finding him? I only pray he will not be hurt and will stay alive till he is found."

He described the whole situation between Antonio and Rachel. All the men looked at each other then looked at Paulo with sympathy. The leader said: "You know that we will try our best, Dr. Molino. Please, just go home and we will continue our search. We promise to call you the minute we know anything."

After he left, the men again looked under every bush, checked every piece of the ground along the wall and made many phone calls. But there was no sign of Antonio, only the sounds of the locusts in the trees and bushes.

Depressed, tired and feeling guilty, Paulo returned home. His wife knelt by the window in the living room, praying and crying softly. He tried to hug her but she not so gently pushed him away. After all, she thought bitterly, he had arrived without Antonio.

Shaken, he handed her Antonio's iPhone, and Sara listened to the message from Rachel. She cried loudly now, unable to control herself. Not knowing how to comfort her, Paulo went to the kitchen to get her a glass of water.

Sara felt like she was a robot on automatic control. Without a thought, she picked up the phone to call Rachel's parents. Then suddenly, the air became filled with a sweet perfume and an odd, warm sensation embraced her. Strangely enough, she was even sure that she was hearing a whisper.

Don't worry; he will be safe.

A gentle silence filled the living room and the wafts of perfume overwhelmed her senses. Sara calmly sat down and looked out the window. Magically, all her anxiety was gone.

When her husband returned and sat down next to her, he noticed the change. She was not crying anymore; in fact, she was smiling. Perplexed at the sudden change, he handed her the glass of water and looked at her expectantly.

"Paulo, somehow I am no longer worried," said Sara, "I heard a soft and strangely familiar whisper telling me that Antonio is safe."

"You heard a strange whisper? Yes! This is *strange* all right!" Paulo exclaimed. "What are you talking about? It's not enough that Antonio is gone and now you have to hallucinate? Listen to me, Sara. Get a hold of yourself! I have enough to worry about!"

Sara would only repeat: "It's okay. I know that he's fine." She looked deeply and sincerely into Paulo's eyes and smiled at him. She gave Paulo a brief embrace. "I'm sorry that I was difficult before. I know it is hard to believe me, but I am convinced of our son's safety." With that comment, she left the room.

Paulo now did the only thing he could think of under the circumstances. He ignored his wife's comments and picked up the phone to dial the Olsenos' number in Laguna Beach. It was Friday afternoon and he knew they would be at home because Roberto worked half a day on Fridays.

"Roberto, it's Paulo. I'm so sorry to disturb you, but I want you to know that Antonio has run away from home, and is on his way to see you."

He paused for a moment, holding back tears. "Antonio left a note for us that he is going to see Rachel." Paulo's voice was breaking up and he stopped talking.

Roberto was shocked, but he tried to remain calm. "Paulo, I can imagine how worried you are, but let's remember we are talking about Antonio. You know that Antonio will be okay; he is athletic, smart, and strong-willed. He will make it across the border and arrive here safely."

"I know you're upset because what Antonio did is wrong, but it is useless to discuss *that* now." Roberto paused for a moment. He thoughtfully continued. "I'm sure he planned everything before he left home. He will be fine and he will be here in no time. Just as soon as he gets here or we hear anything from the authorities I will call you. And we will talk tomorrow anyway."

When they hung up Roberto thought, "I hope what I said to Paulo gave him some comfort; I sincerely believe the boy will be okay." Roberto pondered how to tell his family the news about Antonio. He didn't want his family to worry, especially young Rachel. He sighed. There was nothing to do but tell the truth and face things as a family. He called them all together and told them.

Chapter six

When Antonio opened his eyes the sky was gray and for a brief moment he was disoriented. He reached for his iPhone. Oh, yeah, he had forgotten. It wasn't there. As he touched his clothes something felt funny: Not "laughing" funny, but "really strange" funny.

Then he remembered what he had been wishing for as he fell asleep early yesterday. Chills broke out all over his body. "OMG, did I actually become a locust? I must have; this isn't a dream and I'm not in a movie!" He was shaking. As he reached out to rub the sleepiness out of his eyes, instead of his hand, a bright green large insect leg appeared in front of his eyes. Still thinking he was hallucinating he lifted his other hand; again all he saw was another green leg!

Okaaay! Now what? On the one hand, all he could think about was how much trouble he was in with his family and what a mess he had made of things. What was he going to do? He was truly petrified. On the other hand, he was also almost thirteen, and a guy. "Cool," he said. "I've become an insect and I can fly!" Wait, no sound came out of his lips. He tried talking again. He made a sound of sorts but it sure didn't come from his lips. Antonio, now the locust, began to feel cold all over.

"I can't talk," he screamed. Or he thought he screamed. Only the loud whirr of a locust filled the air. Okay, he thought to himself. At least he could express his thoughts in his *mind*, so that was good. And he had some quick thinking to do.

"I'm not human, and even if I find Rachel she won't know who I am." The whole thing might be cool, but he still shook all the way down to his new insect legs. "Well, I have no choice but to continue my trip. What's the point of going back home? My parents won't know me either. I want to be me again, but how?"

Helplessly he kept staring into the sky waiting for some magic to change him into a human being again. "Please! Oh please! Let me be Antonio again!" His begging was useless and he finally realized it.

"I can't do anything about it, so now I have to concentrate on how I'll get to Laguna Beach. And I can't let myself think about being stuck in the body of an insect forever." He trembled but didn't give up hope. Then the familiar soft laughter filled the air. It almost felt like a super power surrounded him. At that exact moment he became more secure about himself. "There is someone who cares for me. I must have faith that someone is looking over me and that this is all happening for a reason."

He sat down and looked at the sun, which had just begun to peek over the horizon. Spread in front of him for miles and miles were endless green fields, scattered with short trees topped by rounded crown-like branches and bushes full of colorful leaves. It was early morning. He remembered learning in school that locusts slept during the daytime. That must be why he didn't hear their twitters now, as he had last night.

Maybe as a locust he should still be asleep. Whatever! This morning he had no choice but to be awake during the day. And he had no choice but to continue his journey as a locust. He spread his new wings, fluttering them gently and making sure they were strong enough to hold him.

He was surprised at how easy it was to fly. Just in case, he hovered a few inches above the ground. No use tempting fate!

Still very cautious, he circled low and slow, liking the feeling of gliding over the green fields below. Soon he became surer of himself and, as he lifted up with the air currents, he began to fly at high speeds over the hills. "This is great! I can fly so high and so fast; I bet real locusts don't fly like this." Later he would find out he was right: They didn't.

His head was slightly achy and he thought he was getting sick from being so high. He had no idea that there was more magic afoot. Antonio the locust had long antennas right next to his ears and they were pulling him in the *real* direction he needed to be. Once he was back on the right track his headache vanished.

He felt overwhelmed by the sheer power of flying. The view of the mountains and valleys, the birds flying around him, all made him forget that he'd had nothing to eat since he'd become a locust. His mouth was very dry. "I'm not hungry but I *am* thirsty; I guess I have to drink some water." He slowed down while vibrating his wings in place. Just beneath him was a small hill covered in green and gray bushes with brown patches of grass scattered between them.

A few mice were running between the small rocks, and many birds were flying all around. He didn't see anything to drink or eat so he lifted up slightly and then caught sight of something red among the green leaves in the bushes below. They looked like little fruit of some kind.

Cautiously he touched down, his long legs brushing against the moist leaves. He moved very slowly. "This has to be leftover morning dew." He got excited but looked around warily for any predators that might be hungry for him. He waited motionless for a while until it looked like there was nothing to be afraid of.

He bent his new head down to a leaf and to his surprise there were many big drops of water covering it and most of the surrounding leaves. He drank one drop after another until his thirst went away. Feeling better he moved slowly to the red fruit he had spotted from above: It was a small wild strawberry, exactly what he needed to eat. He kept eating until the whole strawberry vanished into his stomach. It was surprising how little a boy locust needed to eat to get full!

Now that he was full, his natural curiosity took over. He really wanted to see what he looked like as a locust. He fluttered his wings and lifted into the air searching for a pond. He knew some places in the desert had small ponds and some of them even had very small fish.

He flew for about an hour. Just as he was beginning to feel tired he got lucky: He found a small pond so clear it almost looked like a mirror. Antonio hovered just above it, fluttering his wings in one spot. He was mesmerized by his image. He couldn't believe what he saw. "Should I laugh or should I cry? I've no idea what to think!" He stared at himself in complete awe.

Now he began to study the incredible image below. Antonio's body was much bigger when compared to a regular locust. He was colored in pale green speckled at the edges with silver dust. He was formed in the shape of a four-inch long bamboo bee—except he was rather plump! Six legs, each two inches long, were curved like human elbows. When the wings were spread, they extended to their full three-inch length and looked like tightly knit green velvet kites.

His head was elongated just like that of a field mouse and his mouth had two fangs on either side. Long green antennas with small silver balls the size of clover buds stuck out of his head. Topping this head were bulging bright red eyes shining like rubies framed with tiny diamonds. "Wow!" He exclaimed. "I kind of think I'm beautiful—in a guy sort of way, of course." He smiled, making fun of himself.

He could feel a great strength in his long legs and claws. His top legs were really more like arms that were attached just below the neck. He wanted to check their strength so he grabbed a branch and effortlessly bent it until it cracked and landed in the pond.

He took a deep breath. "I'm a locust, a large locust; I can fly and I like every minute of it. Has anybody in the world ever had an experience like this?" The feeling was almost mystical. "I wish I could share this with my parents and Rachel. I wish they could see me fly and see how happy I am. I wish they knew that I'm okay. I'm sure they're out of their minds with worry, and here I am having a good time! I'm sorry *Mama* and *Papa.*"

He said it aloud but the only sounds he made were whirring twitters. He understood that he couldn't talk, but he knew he could still think. He remembered something his mom had always told him: "Younger or older, at some point we all fly out of our nest and have to fend for ourselves."

Antonio knew his time to fly had come: He understood that he was on his own.

Chapter seven

Antonio felt that he'd done enough self-admiration and philosophizing to last a lifetime. It was time for action! He took a few sips of water from the lake, spread his wings, rose up high and followed the pull of his antennas. He flew for two hours non-stop. "I'll have to go to sleep soon but before that, I'll have to find something to eat."

He surveyed his surroundings: Everything beneath him looked gray and lifeless. He was glad he had recently had his fill of water. Really tired now, he buzzed down to the first bush he could see. There was nothing on it to eat except a few dry leaves. He decided to skip the paltry meal.

Antonio took a moment to look around. Little birds were singing and jumping from one bush to another. He was glad that locusts were not on their menu! He looked down and saw a group of porcupines digging holes in the ground and moving around playfully. The needles on their backs lay down smoothly so they must feel very safe. Antonio took that as a good sign and decided to take a nap.

The loud whirrs of many locusts woke him up. It was dusk now and suddenly he was wide-awake. "Oh, boy; I've wasted so much time sleeping

instead of flying that I'll never get to Laguna Beach!" He was impatient
with himself. "I won't rest again until I'm at Rachel's house." He took off
quickly but no matter how fast he wanted to fly, his wings had lost their
strength and were slowing him down.

He tried and tried, but he just could not fly: He had no choice but to
rest. As he allowed his drooping wings to lower him, he almost touched
the ground. Antonio then noticed a small green patch and landed on it
without hesitation. Again he checked for predators; he was getting the
hang of this locust thing!

He quickly looked around and saw little yellow flowers glowing in
the dark. "Wow! I'm so lucky; these are dandelions. I remember my mom
used to make delicious salad from the leaves. Thanks, Mom. Now I can
have my dinner, rest for an hour and fly again."

He took a few bites from a green leaf but found that it tasted bitter
without his mom's salad dressing. He ate it anyway to quench his hunger
and thirst. "I guess that even though I look and act like a locust, I'm still
myself inside. Otherwise I wouldn't want salad dressing!" He tried to
chuckle but all he did was twitter.

As he took another bite he suddenly realized something: Maybe some
of the necessary things in life might taste a little bitter but they were
good for you anyway. Not a bad lesson to learn! He was proud of himself.

Antonio thanked his magical companion for the help in finding food
and heard that familiar soft laugh in response. He tried once more for
extra reassurance. "Please, whoever you are, change me back to Antonio
when it is time." But this plea got no response.

The whirrs and twitters of other locusts surrounded him as he
munched. He had his fill and, curious about his locust companions, found
a small branch on a nearby bush from which to watch them. A large
swarm of locusts was eating young grain sprouts growing in a nearby
farm. He understood the locusts' need for food, but felt really badly for
the farmer who was losing his whole crop.

"Maybe there's something I can do that will help both the farmer and the locusts. At least I can give it a try." He buzzed down to the group and chirped, twittered and whirred until he got their full attention. The locusts stopped eating, staring at him. Even though he was much bigger, they recognized Antonio as one of their own and waited to see what he wanted. He fluttered his wings, hovered above them and chirped until they finally followed him.

Antonio lowered himself to the patch of green he had just left, the ground speckled with yellow dandelions and sweet clover. He settled down to munch, hoping his example would work. It did! To his surprise they started munching away at the natural food and chirped merrily along. Happy now, he chirped back at them and watched the locusts enjoying their food to the point that in some places the bare ground began to show. Boy, they sure had a big appetite. He smiled. "Oh, magical power guarding me please let my wish come true: Help the locust to find natural stuff to eat and not the grain sprouts that humans work so hard to plant."

He was glad his transformation into a locust had at least one good result. Now satisfied and no longer tired, he quietly spread his wings and flew in the direction of a white glare of lights off in the distance. He flew for a long while until it became pitch dark and it was evident that the lights were far beyond his immediate reach. He knew he really had to find a safe place to get a few hours of good sleep.

Struggling to see, Antonio landed on a small hill among its tall grasses, some dried and brown and others green and fresh. He settled on a nearby bush, closed his eyes and fell into a deep sleep. When he opened his eyes again, it was almost daybreak. The dark blue of the pre-dawn sky slowly turned into a brilliant blue splendidly highlighted with delicate strokes of peach and pink. Antonio wasted no time in lifting his wings and taking to the sky in flight. He was joined by a flock of small black and brown birds making a symphony of sounds.

After just an hour, the hot rays of the sun beamed forth from beyond the horizon, and the earth became warmer. The birds began to lower themselves gradually to the ground and were lost in the brown hues of the countryside. Antonio continued his flight, no longer accompanied by his small bird companions. He flew until he could see the majestic and mystic mountains ahead, cloaked in a blanket of white fog.

For a moment Antonio stopped and hovered, gazing at the view: He knew there was a very big, very dry desert ahead of him and he had to be ready for the next challenge.

Chapter eight

As he surveyed the view ahead of him, Antonio realized that his first priority should be to find something to eat. Thankfully he also he knew from the National Geographic program he had watched that there should be other desert ponds somewhere near, somewhere in the valley. Naturally curious, he was very excited about having the opportunity to see this incredible desert up close, and explore all of its secrets.

Soon the dry air was stinging his eyes and they became blurry. He had lost track of time and had been acting carefree, depending solely on his antennas for direction on what to do. Now, to his disappointment, the antennas were asleep, making it necessary that he stop. This must mean he was doing something wrong! He knew he had to be responsible for his own actions so he began to aim for the valley. However, almost instantly the air around him became very heavy, his wings moved very slowly and he began to lose his balance. Suddenly he fell down and lost consciousness.

When he woke up, it took Antonio some time to figure out where he was. He felt something very hard underneath him. He lifted his head, and he thought that maybe he was resting on a giant brown mushroom that was cracked all over. He began to move about slowly. Then he noticed the strangest phenomenon. "This thing is moving with me!" he exclaimed. "Where am I? What is this big shell doing here?" He hopped to the very edge of it, and started to laugh hysterically, his laugh echoing through the whole valley.

"Imagine: All this time I was sleeping on a desert turtle, and riding on it. If I continue like this and at this speed, I'll never get to Laguna Beach!" He laughed at himself again.

When he finally became serious, the realization hit him. "I was punished for not taking responsibility for myself; I'm so lucky I'm still alive." Now he felt guilty. "From now on, I'll watch for every sign my body gives me, for if I don't then I will really be hurt." He wanted to resume his flying but his wings refused to open.

Antonio was sure he was dehydrated and he had to find something to drink and eat immediately. He jumped off the turtle, his hop wobbly. He struggled to reach a bush, which at least would give him some shade even though it looked dry and fruitless.

He sat there, breathing heavily, watching the birds scrambling under other bushes. With a great effort he moved towards the birds. "Wow, I'm so lucky again!" He saw black berries that smelled like juniper on a nearby bush and wobbled towards it. With his hooked arm he grabbed the branch, lowered it to his mouth, and chewed on the bittersweet berries one after another.

Feeling stronger, he decided to linger there, and watched something moving under the other bush full of fruit. His eyes focused. "Wow, a chipmunk!" he exclaimed. "And it's eating the berries, too." The chipmunk was indeed dining, sitting on his tail, holding a branch between his two paws while he chewed on the berries.

Antonio was fascinated by the furry dark animal that seemed to be enjoying the food while his little eyes darted around. The chipmunk then noticed Antonio, got closer and tried playfully to reach Antonio with his paw, but just in time Antonio started to hop away. To his surprise, his locust wings spread, and he was able to fly away and nestle on a nearby bush, where the chipmunk couldn't reach him.

Antonio sat there enjoying a few bites from a juicy berry, and again thinking how dangerous his fall had been. "I'm so lucky I'm alive," he repeated. The locust screams echoed in the valley. The sun was rising higher and Antonio knew he should be flying, but somehow his wings were still heavy. He spotted a tall trunk nearby with one branch full of leaves. He flew up to it with a great deal of effort, settled in the shade of those green leaves and once again fell asleep.

The loud chirping of a large black bird woke him up. He quickly jumped out of the way of its big beak. His heart was beating so fast he could hardly catch his breath. He was no longer sleepy! He tried his wings again, circled around, lifted higher and to his delight, he began to fly without any effort. His antennas with their tiny satellites were leading him, he hoped, to Laguna Beach.

After a while, in order not to make the same mistake as before, he felt he needed to find food and water. He glanced down and everything *looked* brown but he knew that somewhere there had to be water and the berry bushes. Slowing down, he lowered his fatigued body, his wings again moving in slow motion. But this time he didn't fall.

Then, as if from nowhere, the big black bird he had seen before appeared flying just next to him. Antonio, cleverly thinking of a free ride and no longer afraid of the bird, lifted himself higher and landed on the bird's back. He fastened his hooked arms to the bird's feathers and promptly fell asleep.

When he woke up, he felt rested and knew that he had travelled a great distance on the back of the big bird. He was happy to see other birds, almost his size, just below him, flying from one bush to another. He jumped off the bird's back and settled on the tallest of the bushes, examining the branches. To his surprise, on even these almost dry branches, very dark berries flourished.

One small bird was sitting on the lowest branch poking at a berry with an unusually long red beak. In fact, the whole bird was unusual. His tail was longer than that of other birds, his claws were very long and crescent-shaped and his wings were scattered with red feathers.

Antonio glanced at him suspiciously for a while and then, feeling safe, settled in for a meal of juniper bush berries. He found that he really enjoyed their taste. This time the aroma of the fruit was so strong that it reminded him of the aroma of juniper incense used in the church he attended with his parents.

As he continued eating the berries he thought of home, family and friends, forgetting about the unusual red beaked bird staring at him. He told himself to move on. If he stayed, he would continue to think of home and that would weaken his resolve. He wasn't hungry anymore so he flew to another more comfortable branch. He looked around to distract himself and was glad to see the friendly bird still in the same place and still looking at him.

"He should be my inspiration; here he is living his life all alone as a bird and he's okay. He has no hope to change and yet he is happy as he is. This is another lesson to learn."

"I *do* have hope to change back to being human," he reflected. "But even if I never get to change from being a locust to being a person for the rest of my life, it would still be worth all the sacrifice just to see Rachel. I could always stay in her garden and see her every day through her window!"

He smiled mischievously.

Chapter nine

Rachel sat in her bedroom looking out the window at the garden. As soon as she had finished her homework–English grammar, history and geometry–her mind had begun to wander to thoughts of Antonio. She was so worried about him leaving the comfort of his home in Mexico; she thought he'd been very foolish to risk his life this way. Now, no one knew where he was or even if he was still alive! Ever the optimist, Rachel willed herself to think positive thoughts. She wouldn't allow anything to make her think Antonio would not make it to America.

She put on the TV just to watch the news. Every day she expected to hear something about Antonio, but again there was nothing. Suddenly she became very anxious and began to cry, all her positive vibes gone. With her body trembling from sheer frustration, she thought, "Maybe I'll never see Antonio again; maybe something dreadful has happened to him." Rachel decided to call Antonio's mom, Sara, for some reassurance. At the end of their conversation Sara said, "Even though there is no trace of Antonio on either the Mexican or the American border, I *know* Antonio is okay. He is strong, young and smart, and I assure you he will soon be on your doorstep."

Talking to Sara had given Rachel a bit of much needed inspiration but the cheerfulness didn't last very long: Rachel was just having a very bad day. She decided to pick up a book to read but, after half an hour went by, she still couldn't concentrate on it. She was just sitting on the floor, resting her chin on her knees as she hugged them close to her body to give herself comfort. Rachel looked around the room mindlessly: To her sad eyes, the beautiful and cheery room had become a place full of gloom.

The pale pink bedspread was decorated with a few colorful pillows. Two dolls and a stuffed white poodle nestled among the pillows, representing her cherished childhood memories. The room was a comfortable place to study, with its white desk and chair in one corner, books scattered over the surface of the desk. The other corner held the dresser and drawers full of memories and clothes. Thankfully the large closet was now closed. It was better that way since the closet was in dire need of some order, but lately Rachel had no energy for organizing.

On the pale pink wall in front of her was a large framed photo of her class in the seventh grade in Mexico. She glanced at the image of Antonio smiling, his spiky hair shining and framing his handsome face. He looked like he had not one worry in the world! Rachel was standing next to Antonio; her almond shaped face with the golden tan was framed with long sun-kissed hair. Her bright eyes and beautiful smile sparkled off the photo. She sighed. Those were very happy times. Even now, although she had made many friends in her new home, she really missed Antonio and her friends back in Mexico. She never said anything about Antonio to any of her friends here; she thought they just wouldn't understand.

Rachel felt more tears fill her eyes. She sighed again. "So many changes!" she thought. "But to tell the truth, I can't feel sorry for myself; I feel sorry for Antonio, not knowing where he is, what he's eating and where he's sleeping."

Rachel was glad her mom was not home yet from the office because she didn't want to worry her mom with these tears. She kind of gave up on thinking about things. She slowly walked to her bed, lay down and curled up on it with Cookie, her reddish, furry cat at her feet. Instantly she fell asleep.

Chapter ten

Rachel's mom, Juliette, came home from the office. As she opened the door, she called out, "Rachel!" After calling out several times without an answer, Juliette glanced at her watch. "It's five-thirty; so she can't be at softball practice. I wonder what's going on." Alexander was still at his soccer practice, so no use calling for him.

As she walked through the long hallway, Juliette glanced in the mirror. Her white uniform fit well and accentuated her tall slender figure. Her face was almond shaped just like Rachel's, and her hair was the same length and sun-kissed color. They were both lucky to have healthy heavy hair! More and more they looked so much alike. She smiled and puckered her lips just as Rachel did when she wanted to be funny. Juliette had to make dinner, but first she wanted to see what Rachel was doing and give her the usual afternoon hug.

Juliette grabbed the doorknob, pushed the door open and was surprised to find Rachel asleep on top of the bedspread. Concerned, she walked to her daughter, sat down on the edge of the bed and whispered softly, "How are you Rachel?" Cookie raised his head and stared at Juliette with wise green eyes. Rachel lifted her puffy eyelids and Juliette instantly knew there was something wrong: Her daughter never slept after school. Instead she played softball and practiced piano.

"Rachel, is anything wrong?" Juliette felt her forehead. "You don't have a fever. What's going on?" Suddenly Rachel threw her arms around her mother's neck and tearfully began to talk about her worries. As Juliette held Rachel close and made comforting sounds, Alexander walked in. His mother gave him a sign with her hand to be quiet.

He tiptoed into the room, trying to make as little noise as possible, his tall thin body still clad in green shorts and tee shirt of the same color, With the capital "A" on the front. He sat down on the small, upholstered, white chair in the corner and watched both of them. His round face was accentuated with happy green eyes and a perky nose and perpetually sparkled with a quick smile and funny expressions.

Juliette was very concerned about both Rachel and Antonio. No news about Antonio frightened her, but she couldn't upset Rachel any more then she already was. As Juliette began to comfort Rachel, Alexander interrupted. He stood up, walked to Rachel and hugged her with that happy grin on his face. "Rachel, you know how strong and determined Antonio is, so don't worry, he'll make it. I wish I could be with him; it would be so much fun!" His mother gave him a scornful look. He ignored it and continued anyway. "Rachel, there are so many illegal immigrants coming here, all of them made it and you know that they're not as physically fit and clever as Antonio. Don't worry, I can't wait to see him and hear all about his adventures."

Rachel's first thoughts were that her younger brother had lost his mind. "No surprise there," she reflected. Nevertheless, as she stared at him, his enthusiasm became contagious. He was making funny faces and soon she started to laugh. The siblings settled on her bed and began talking and laughing, wondering how Antonio had managed to outsmart everybody at both borders.

Juliette, both surprised and pleased at seeing the drama turn into a comedy, left the room to change her clothes. "The resilience of youth," she thought and walked to the kitchen to make dinner. Soon her husband's office would close and he would walk in the door. Although she continued to worry about Antonio, the two kids upstairs lifted her spirits, and she couldn't wait to tell Roberto about them.

She opened the sliding door to the patio, lit the barbeque, pulled a few steaks and corn on the cob from the refrigerator to place on the grill, and filled two high stem glasses with cool drinks. She sat down on the lounge in the patio and waited for her husband.

Juliette almost called Antonio's parents, but she needed Roberto to be with her when she did. Since pessimism never entered his mind, he had a very calming effect on people. Juliette reflected on how alike Roberto and Alexander were both in appearance and character. She loved them so very much! Her thoughts wandered and she began to think about how fortunate she was with her family. For all their sakes she really hoped that Antonio would arrive safely. She was hopeful that his parents, their dear friends, would find a way to follow him legally: She missed them too.

Chapter eleven

Right on schedule Roberto, Rachel's father, walked in through the kitchen door and strolled directly to the patio where he embraced Juliette. He reached for the glasses, handed one to her and smiled. "I'm so glad it's the weekend. This felt like a very long week at the office. Somehow spring every year makes so many people sick."

He kicked off his white shoes, sat down comfortably next to her and, with a deep sigh of relief, took a long sip of the tasty drink. "How are you and the kids? It's so quiet here today." Juliette gave him a smile, but not her usual one.

"Okay," he said, "What's wrong? You seem to be so unhappy." Juliette clasped her long-fingered hands in the special way she had when she was upset and began to talk non-stop about Antonio, Rachel and Alexander.

Roberto listened thoughtfully. After he absorbed it all, his face showed controlled concern. He glanced far into the distance as Juliette watched him, not knowing what to make of his silence. He took another sip, lifted himself from the seat, took her hands and pulled her up. He embraced her tightly and smiled his usual warm smile.

"I love the boy and I give him credit for his courage and initiative, but I'll be happy when I see him here. I'm sure he'll make it since he's very smart and independent, but I still worry about him." After that comment he ended the embrace and walked slowly to the kitchen with his head down, where he picked up the telephone and dialed Antonio's parents in Cocobana, Mexico.

No one was home so he left a short message. "Hello friends, it's Roberto." He paused then continued. "Paulo, don't worry, Antonio will make it, he is young and strong. Don't be angry with him; as we know young love doesn't understand what the rules are! I will call you later, and as I said to you before, he will be fine." That weekend the Olseno family did not discuss the subject again.

On Monday morning, as he did every weekday, Roberto dropped off the children at school, with Juliette following him to the office one hour later. She opened the front door of the house and, on the top step, she found a tiny furry dog staring at her with large soulful black eyes. His nose was shaped like a big black olive; his long fur was dark ash in color but clumped together from dirt and neglect.

Juliette's heart was touched and she immediately picked him up and rushed to the car. The first thing that came to her mind was to get some help. "I will stop on my way to the office at the vet, and ask her to take care of the puppy and feed him." Only later did she think to ask the vet's office to find out if someone had lost a pet. After a brief examination, the vet looked at the puppy and said, "From what I see, this poor thing is clearly homeless. Do you want to adopt him?"

"Yes, yes I do; I already love him!" Juliette replied, her eyes sparkling with emotion. The vet smiled in return. "I am so glad you will keep him, Dr. Olseno. Just come by on your way home today and you can pick him up. He will be clean, vaccinated and ready for your family to love."

Juliette left very excited. "This little one is a miracle! He will bring some happiness and distraction to our home at this difficult time."

Chapter twelve

The sun sat high and heavy above the horizon. Antonio was flying just over the top of the mountains, admiring the world below that looked so big and wide with just a few clouds scattered here and there. Amid the backdrop of a cobalt blue sky, the mountains seemed gray and unfriendly. Yet he remained excited to be able to enjoy this special view from the top.

The mountains were rocky, speckled with clusters of ash colored grass. The valley far below was covered in large stones of different shapes and sizes with scattered burgundy bushes holding on bravely between them. Antonio flew in for a closer look. A few very small gray birds about the same size as Antonio circled just above the valley. Below and alone, a large ominous-looking black bird sat on a bush scratching at something with his long beak.

The bird's featherless head sat on a body over a foot long, his pink skin wrinkled and bumpy. This bird was not going to win the prize for being the most beautiful in the desert! Antonio stared at the yellow eyes that bulged out of the bird's homely face, noting how alert they seemed.

"Hey," thought Antonio, "this is the same bird I already took ride on! Is he following me?"

Antonio flew in even closer to get a good look at his former ride. He was amazed to be able to identify the bird out of the picture book in his biology class. This ugly guy was a vulture! "OMG! I took a ride on a vulture! What was I thinking?"

Antonio knew that this bird could eat anything and never get sick because he was resistant to infections and bacteria. The bird could fly non-stop for five hundred miles and still not get tired. He stared at the bird's large body and noticed that it looked over-weight. "How could he fly with me on his back?" Antonio wondered. The vulture stared back. "This guy can't be trusted," Antonio realized with shock. "He would eat me just as a small snack!"

Antonio lost no time in getting his locust wings to fly him far away from the ferocious bird. Taking a quick look behind, he realized that the large bird was indeed following him. Now what could he do? The vulture was so close that Antonio trembled from fright. This was no time to be afraid! To escape him Antonio started to circle up, down and around him repeatedly, diving and coming back up. Suddenly he lost his fear and began to have fun! Antonio laughed aloud, his locust sounds echoing through the valley.

The loud sounds made the vulture really try to catch the locust. His big beak was open, his huge wings were moving slower, and every time he got closer to Antonio he moved more slowly and with more purpose. After a while, Antonio made a few twists around to confuse the vulture and ended up actually landing on the bird's back, fastening his locust claws on its feathers! The vulture kept flying, not even noticing the extra weight.

Suddenly Antonio felt strangely safe and secure. It was as if that wonderful unexplained power that had been helping him all along on his journey once more took over and banished all his fears. He realized that this unseen power had brought the vulture to him to make the trip safer and shorter. Now even his antennas seemed to enjoy the ride. He felt the antennas become alert, pulling, turning and magically making the vulture fly in the right direction!

Antonio couldn't help himself; he was so happy that he started to laugh aloud and sing his favorite song repeatedly: "Baby, Baby!" If only Justin Bieber could hear him now! "Oh, wait! Maybe not!" He could only imagine how loud and annoying his locust sounds actually were, since all the nearby birds quickly flew away, scattering in every direction.

Antonio felt powerful and in total control. "This ride has surely shortened my trip to Laguna Beach. I wish Rachel could see me now; she wouldn't worry anymore." Flying free on the vulture's back for a few hours, he was happy and thankful for the break.

As the day passed the temperature became hotter and the air grew even drier. The vulture started to lower his flight pattern, aiming for a place to land. Antonio noticed the descent and decided to get off while the getting was good! He very carefully let his claws go loose, and to confuse and escape the vulture, dropped down as fast as he could.

He landed on a fan palm, surrounded by clustered bushes full of black berries and sighed with relief. "I'm so lucky that these are the same berries I ate before," he noted. Many small brown and black birds with tiny beaks were chirping joyfully and eating the berries, jumping from one bush to another.

Antonio also jumped onto a bush. Using his new locust expertise, he grabbed a branch full of berries with his clawed hands, dipped his mouth into one berry, then another, and slowly drank the juice while chewing on the pulp with great hunger. He was extra careful to watch for the vulture, but luckily, the large bird had gone to the other side of the valley.

The sun was slowly dipping down over the horizon. It was late afternoon yet Antonio wanted to travel more miles before it got dark. He tried to move his wings but they felt heavy so he realized that he had no choice but to stay around for a while. "Maybe I'll have to spend the night here," he thought. On that note he closed his eyes and tried to sleep, but confused thoughts kept him awake.

"If I sleep now, my trip will take much longer," he kept thinking. After a while he tried to take off again, but the wings wouldn't budge. "Okay, I guess it's clear that I have to listen to my body telling me I need to rest." He jumped from the bush to the ground, found a bunch of dry leaves, made a nest of them and pushed himself underneath the pile to escape the heat and become invisible to the birds and other predators.

Since he wasn't sleepy he just looked around at his surroundings and again felt like shouting with excitement and gratitude. "I'm so lucky to be alive!" he sang. His locust scream came out on impulse and frightened birds lifted into the air like one dark cloud. "I'm so sorry; it was selfish of me to scream this way," he said to them. But they were gone.

As he looked around he noticed that one of the birds had not flown away. The little bird was just sitting on the ground under a nearby bush, intently looking towards where Antonio nestled.

Antonio wasn't sure if the bird had really noticed him under the bunch of dry leaves, but he decided to stay a little longer anyway and wait until the sun went down. It would be cooler and he would have more strength to fly. It would also be safer.

Being a bird watcher with his father back home, Antonio realized that he had never seen this kind of small bird before. The bird was really kind of cute. It had a red beak over an inch long that was curved in the shape of a crescent. Its unusual tail was long and pink, looking strangely like an old-fashioned lace lady's fan. The bird stood around three inches tall and his feathers were a blend of grey speckled with red. There was no pink on his body, only on his tail.

"What a strange looking bird," Antonio thought. Then he realized that the bird must have been thinking the same about him, with his oversized locust body. They both sat there for a long time, staring at each other.

☙❧

Chapter thirteen

After a long while, the two creatures declared a sort of truce, and each drifted off into a short nap. Finally, although it was not yet night, the blazing orange sun began to touch the outlined horizon and it instantly became cooler in the desert valley.

It was time for Antonio to slip out of the nest. He flipped his wings, sat comfortably on a nearby branch and dipped his mouth in the juniper berries again; He hungrily sipped the bittersweet juice. "From now on I'll only eat juniper; it gives me energy and it makes me feel good, and now I know that it won't make my little locust body sick."

As he sipped and slurped berries, Antonio looked for his bird companion: Sure enough, the little bird with the big red beak was still there, sitting in the same spot. After all this time of mutual admiration, Antonio now felt he had made a friend on this journey. He decided to call his new friend "Red".

It was time to go and get in some more flight time before total darkness arrived. Antonio glanced over at Red one last time and, with a slight ache in his heart, knew that he had to leave the little guy behind.

"Perhaps we'll find one another again," he chirped in good-bye. He spread his wings and lifted into the sky.

The time for play had ended. Suddenly, whenever he made a movement in the wrong direction, his antennas pulled at him with a force that hurt his head so badly that he had to follow the pull instantly. It was as if his magical overseer was telling him to buckle down and get the job done.

Still somewhat puzzled by the whole situation he kept asking himself: "Who's doing this to me?" Of course there were no answers. He could hear the magical soft laugh just above him, but he thought it was all in his head from being tired. Anyway, he didn't know anymore what reality was and what it wasn't; he was living in a fantasy world for now.

His wings were slowing down which meant he had to stop some place. After his long yet fast flight, the day was quickly ending and the sky looked like it was set on fire. Soon the sun would completely vanish, only to shine somewhere else. Antonio was fascinated with the beauty around him. Brush-like strokes of red, orange, blue and white painted the horizon and spread up into the sky. With each beautiful dusk he was very happy to be getting closer to Rachel's home.

"Somehow I'll get to see Rachel, and somehow I'll become Antonio again," he affirmed to himself. "Whoever changed me into the locust must have had a reason for it. I hope when the time comes he or she will have mercy on me and will transform me back into the real Antonio. Maybe my current hardships will win me a happy ending." He prayed, "Oh my Guardian Angel, please be with me and never leave me. I will never do anything to disobey you and my parents again."

Gliding through the deepening twilight he glanced down to see the varied flora of the earth. He noticed the ever-changing green hues of different grasses and bushes, and the trees of all different colors and sizes.

He slowed the movements of his wings and gradually tried to find a safe place to land, eat something and browse around. He heard the loud sound of an airplane very high in the air and thought, "I'm happy to be able to fly, too! This is something that no one else has ever done! I'm almost sure of that. Ha! Ha! Ha!"

Now he was flying very close to the ground. He noticed large cactuses in clumps spread over a pebble-covered hill. Yuck! Mice and rats were running in all directions away from a long brown snake spiraling its way between the dry leaves. Antonio shivered at the thought of being near that snake, and even the rats.

He picked the tallest cactus to land on. As he touched down, he felt a tiny pinch on his belly, but he didn't pay much attention to it. He'd been hurt many times playing soccer and picking things up on field trips and had never had problems before; this was just a pinch. Seeing nothing else available, he decided to put aside his earlier resolve to eat only juniper berries and try something different to eat. He would munch on some cactus.

Once he felt comfortable sitting atop the white cactus flowers, he dipped his tongue into the flesh of the cactus and very soon was sipping the tasteless liquid. Not too delicious, but it would do for now.

The glare of the full moon soon gave him enough light to find a safe place to sleep, but wherever he looked all he could see were the mice and rats playing and running around. Then he remembered the snake. Maybe he should go a little higher to find a place to rest!

In the background he heard the lonely wails of coyotes and the soft chirps of birds settling down for the night amid the ever-present cries of the locust. Realizing he didn't have much choice of venue, he flew up the side of a tree near its trunk. He found a comfortable branch, curled his wings under as close as possible to his body, flipped onto his back and watched the moon slowly move across the cloudless sky.

Chapter fourteen

Antonio's belly began to itch during the night and he woke up. Of course he ignored the irritation: He might be a locust on the outside, but he was still a teenage boy on the inside! At first he didn't pay much attention to the painful prickle, thinking it would go away. Then he decided he was wrong about it going away but he couldn't do anything about it anyway, so he might as well ignore it. Finally, he became determined to fly as far as he could and get as close to Rachel as possible, or at least as close to people as possible, in spite of the itch. That this wouldn't help him *feel* any better never occurred to him; at least it was something to do.

He whirred loudly, lifted as high as he could and flew wherever the antennas pulled his head. At some point during flight he realized that he must have been hurt by the prick from the cactus. So much for acquired toughness due to soccer practice and field trips!

The itch soon turned into a burning sensation over his entire belly that made him feel like he was on fire. Now he was frightened and his antennas drooped and pulled him down. He knew the drill: When this occurred it was necessary to land quickly. As he zoomed in closer to the ground, he noticed a large red circle below that looked just like a pillow in the soft moonlight.

Antonio decided to go in for an emergency landing. As he reached the surface it felt very cool, comfortable and smooth: Exactly what he was looking for. He lay down, took a few deep breaths, folded his wings close to his body and fell asleep. He slept for a long while and his sleep was deep and healing.

Abruptly, a very small but persistent movement underneath his wings shook him awake and into the throes of his worst nightmare! Above him the large fangs of a snake stood ready to pierce his face. He screamed very loudly while simultaneously trying to fly. "Oh, no!" he thought, "This is hopeless!" Then, miraculously, out of nowhere, his friend Red appeared.

Red used all his power to fly at the menacing fangs, pushing Antonio away and off the snake and propelling him into the sky. The bird and the locust made a strange pair as they both chirped loudly and rapidly flew into the sky and away from the bite of the snake. Antonio flew as quickly as his little wings could take him, which, under the circumstances, was quite far! Secure in the company of his new friend and hero he turned around to thank him, but Red was gone.

Antonio couldn't believe he had lost Red again. "Where are you?" he cried. Only other locusts around him answered his loud query. "I guess I'm alone again," Antonio cried mournfully. The other birds flying near him fluttered away urgently at the piercing sounds of his whirrs and trills.

This time Antonio really felt the long, sad pull of true loneliness: He missed his home, his family and his friends. Soon he was feeling very sorry for himself as he had at the beginning of his journey, and tears blinded his little ruby eyes. His antennas drooped and his wings sputtered. He sighed his mournful locust wail.

Then unexpectedly that soft laugh vibrated in the air above him. The gentle laugh reminded him that he was loved and assured him he was not alone: He finally resolved to stop feeling sorry for himself. He gave himself a strong mental shake: "I have to be strong; I can't cry, that won't help me," he determined.

Antonio picked up his speed and after only half an hour green fields appeared below him.

Chapter fifteen

More relaxed now, he flew lower and closer into the valley below. To his surprise he could see people moving between the green trees! Finally! He was so happy that he zoomed in for a closer look. Ahead some men were bending and others standing, all dressed in the typical garb of the Mexican *campesino*: Light colored long-sleeved shirts, gray pants and dark shoes, with large *sombreros* shading their faces. They were bending and picking at a large crop of strawberries.

Antonio realized that even though the men looked just like the Mexican workers back home, they were indeed on the American side of the border. He'd come upon a work crew of farmers, typical of the nearby Southern California agricultural towns. He knew that many Mexicans had come to America to work the fields, as well as live and work in the cities.

Antonio was so grateful to see people that he exclaimed, "Oh my Guardian Angel, thank you for leading me to people at last! Please let me become one of them again." He closed his eyes then opened them, one at a time. He looked at where his arms and legs should be and still saw claws. Oh, well! He realized he still looked like a large locust; the wish didn't come true. Disappointed but happy to be with people again, he landed on a large strawberry bush very close to one of the men, as the man picked at the lush red strawberries and placed them in a basket.

The man's face was sunburned, he had creases around his eyes and mouth that showed the effects of the sun and a life lived with a perpetual smile. His hair was dark and his eyes shone with intent as he sang a lusty rendition of a song that Antonio knew well. The song was written by Raul de Blasio and called *"Mexico, Mexico"*. The lyrics reminded Antonio of home in a happy way and he sat on the branch intently listening to the words.

Of course, the worker had no way of knowing that this extra-large locust perched on the branch nearby was really a Mexican young man. He noticed Antonio and stopped singing. Pointing to the locust he said. "Look at that rascal, *muchachos*: I wish I could be like him—free to fly around the world and never work!"

Antonio gulped. The man just made the same wish that Antonio had made at the beginning of his journey! Antonio closed his eyes and waited for the transformation to occur. He opened his eyes. The man was still there; he had *not* become a locust. What happened? Well, obviously nothing, he thought. Maybe this magic thing only worked for boys! On the other hand, maybe it worked only for him and only in one direction. OMG!

The men continued to speak in Spanish, laughing and making fun of each other. They mimicked the funny way they were forced to walk after bending low picking the fields all day. Antonio marveled at their sense of fun and how they were able to joke about their hard work. He remembered what his parents had always taught him: It didn't matter what type of work you had to do in life; all work was good and honorable. These men had certainly learned that lesson well!

Then the men sat down to take a break. The man who Antonio now thought of as the leader, and who had just been singing, said in a scratchy voice, "I feel very lucky to be in America. Look at us, we all have jobs, our families are happy, our children go to school. To tell the truth I would not want to live in any other country."

He paused for a moment, stood up and spread his arms as if to hug his surroundings. "It is so beautiful here, and the weather is always nice. I have always wished to bring my parents here, but they are too old." He swallowed hard. "Just to make up for the fact that I'm not near them, I send them a check every chance I get."

The other men nodded in agreement; they were not surprised to hear this since they all had done the same thing. One of them said, "We found our happiness here, and we have to share it in some way with our parents." The men got up to work again.

Antonio understood how they felt and really wished he could talk to them. "I miss Mexico and my parents, too," he cried, wanting to join the conversation, "but I also want to live in this country!" Unfortunately, Antonio had forgotten that his "talking" now sounded more like cries, twitters and wails. The more he tried to talk, the louder the noise he made.

The noise became so loud that all of the men dropped their strawberries to the ground, put their hands to their ears, and looked at each other in confusion. "What in the heavens was that?" A few of them started to turn over strawberry leaves looking for the source of the noise but found nothing. One of them joked: "As long as it is not a coyote I don't care!"

Suddenly, the air became loaded with swarms of big black flies that began to buzz around them. The more the men waved their arms to get them off, the more the flies kept coming back. One man said, "They are as good as a clock. These flies always come at the same time, and when they do, it means it's time to go home!" They carried the last baskets full of strawberries to the truck and drove away.

Antonio glanced after them a little jealously as they drove away: He also wanted to be going home in America. "Too bad they don't live in the direction where I'm going; I could've hitched a ride and helped them sing a few songs!" he thought.

He laughed at his own joke, his locust cries echoing in the now silent field.

Chapter sixteen

Now Antonio was left alone with only the big flies as companions. He feasted on a strawberry, chewing slowly, enjoying the sweetness. Then he flew up to a palm tree with fan-like branches, sat down on a bunch of red seeds attached to the trunk and fell asleep in its sparse shade.

When he opened his eyes the pain in his tummy was worse, much worse. "Oh, boy," he thought. "The darn itch is back." He felt hot, cold, and achy. He thought he might have an infection and got really scared when he started to feel the chills.

He was surrounded by the usual little birds chirping happily around him, yet he felt completely alone and with no energy to fly. Very frightened now, he hid under the palm leaf and waited for the pain to go away. The pain worsened instead: Antonio really didn't know what to do so he just sat and worried.

As he was running out of hope, he looked down at another palm frond just below and was surprised to see his lost friend, Red. "I'm so happy to see you again and I need your help so badly!" Soft locust whispers came out of Antonio's mouth as he gasped with very little strength, "Are you here to rescue me again? I hope so!"

The little bird held in his red beak a small piece of healing aloe plant, its thick liquid dripping. He hopped up to the branch next to his locust friend, placed the aloe piece near Antonio with the wet side up, and chirped. Antonio didn't move so Red chirped again. This time Antonio got the message. Trusting his little friend, Antonio crawled over to the aloe sprig and lay down on his belly across its surface. The aloe felt cool and soothing against his tummy; soon Antonio became drowsy and fell into a deep sleep.

Red flew in circles around Antonio until he was sure his friend had closed his eyes. Then Red fluttered over to a tall tree next to the palm and settled in to wait. He nestled quietly into the groove between the big branches of the tree and took a curious look around the area.

He was happy to see that there was plenty of food for both of them: Strawberries, other plants and even leftover crumbs of bread and cookies from the men who had worked the field. Red ate some, making sure there would be enough left over for Antonio when he woke up.

Antonio opened his heavy lids. At first he didn't remember where he was and then as he looked around he recalled the strawberry fields, the men who had worked there, and how sick he had gotten. Finally he remembered that Red had come back to help him! Red, what a wonderful friend, but who was he, anyway? Antonio chirped, and as he moved, he noticed his belly had no more pain and the chills were gone. The aloe had worked, and there was even food for him to eat: A stash of small strawberries and cookie crumbs were displayed on a leaf next to him. He ate his fill and felt great for the first time in a long while.

Now he started thinking about Red. Antonio was sure the strange little bird with the red beak had brought him the food as well as taking care of his bellyache. How strange! Now Red had vanished again into his mystery world.

Antonio continued to be very puzzled. "Who is Red? Is it possible that he's human too? Was he changed into a bird, just like I'm changed into a locust?" He couldn't stop thinking about it.

It was getting dark. Antonio was still sitting in the same spot with his head down, thinking through the mystery of Red when all of a sudden thoughts of his parents and Rachel came to mind. "I should have listened to Rachel and waited for my parents to immigrate! How badly they all must feel right now: Rachel, my family, even Mario, my soccer friend. I miss them all. I'm just the worse kind of guy."

His head spun with all the confusing thoughts that he hadn't allowed himself to think about recently and his spirits were really down. All of a sudden his nose began to twitch and he sneezed. But he wasn't sick again; his little nose was twitching from detecting a distinct aroma. It was that fragrance he had first noted when he was transformed into a locust back on the big wall. The perfume, just like the magical soft laugh, made him feel immediately hopeful and at peace: He once again knew that someone, somehow, was watching over him.

Antonio mustered his courage: His goal was to reach Rachel and that was what he was going to do! While he sat there musing, it had become fully dark. He glanced at the moon covered by a thin veil of a wispy white cloud. The beauty, the magic, all of it, gave him energy and inspiration; it was once again time to move on.

Chapter seventeen

Antonio decided to travel by the light of the moon. Spreading his wings he flew high into the evening sky; in the far distance he spotted a long line of electric lights decorating the horizon. Flying higher than any bird, he sped up the pace, hoping to soon reach the brightly lit city.

He spoke to the magic power again: "Whoever you are, please lead me to Laguna Beach! Help me to be human again and I promise that I'll never do anything stupid again." He realized that he should have listened to Rachel: Now he had to move forward and continue to ask for help and guidance.

Antonio knew his geography, so he had a feeling he was now hovering above the Mojave Desert. He zoomed in for a better view of the local fauna and flora. The glare of the moon soon highlighted a mirror-like stream, crossing the desert hills dotted with a multitude of trees and bushes.

He could hear the howls of coyotes echoing through the night. Various night birds and insects were humming, squeaking and chirping. Antonio hovered above it all, taking in all the details. All of a sudden boyish enthusiasm took over: He had an idea! "Wow! Wouldn't it be really great to check out a ghost town? What was the name of the one around here that was so famous? Calico, I think it's called Calico."

He slowed down the movements of his wings even more, passed over the top of a mountain and began to fly much lower. No wonder the area was called Calico: Even in the dark he could see patches of red, blue, green, yellow and vermillion below as a long narrow valley magically appeared ahead of him, and he spotted the ghost town!

His ruby red eyes were shining like the lens of a camera as he landed on a small square building constructed of big gray blocks of stone. It had high openings instead of a door. He really hoped that someone would be inside. "How cool is this? How great would it be to share this with my teacher and the kids at school?"

Two rusty four-wheeled carriages stood in front of the building. He circled around, made a left turn, flew in, and found himself in a square room with heavy stone walls. Scattered below were numerous rats and mice apparently searching for something and scratching the floor playfully.

"OMG, this has to be the best part of my trip; I'm so glad to be here, and it's a full moon so I can see everything. I've got to see at least one ghost."

He now looked up at the ceiling and grinned, blinking his bright eyes; something was making weird hissing noises. He looked up. Way cool! Dozens of creepy gray bats hung motionless from the heavy decomposing wood beams. He settled down in the groove between two gray stones up high and took in the whole scenario. Fascinating! It was just after midnight.

Suddenly, he heard strange human screams outside; maybe there really would be ghosts tonight! He held his breath in anticipation. Two ragged figures ran through the opening, screaming and pulling at each other's long tangled hair. The bigger one pushed the smaller one down to the floor with great force and dragged the unfortunate being over the uneven surface made up of small, sharp and broken stones.

Both of their scary faces were covered with scratches, dried blood and oily lumps. Their gray clothes were torn and tattered, ragged pieces flying around their bodies. They didn't look like real people, they looked like—no, it couldn't be: They looked like zombies! These were no ordinary ghosts; these were the cool zombies that were the latest craze!

The big zombie screamed. "You took my biggest chunk of silver a long time ago. I remember you, you devil. Now you'll pay for it or I'll strangle you with my bare hands."

Grabbing the little zombie's narrow throat, he fastened his big scruffy hands around him. Gurgling sounds were coming from the small zombie's throat and his worn-out body was bent over in pain. The big zombie was laughing so loud that even the bats flew away in fear.

Antonio couldn't take the craziness anymore; he felt sorry for the little zombie. He hurled himself at the big one's head, digging sharp locust claws into his skull. Then he flew back up to his hiding place to observe.

The big zombie let go of the small one in a hurry, grabbing his own head and screaming. "Who did that to me? So help me, if I find you I will kill you right now, you rat!"

Not a rat at all, Antonio was thinking. He gave a long locust chirp, laughing, again waiting to see what would happen next.

The big zombie looked at his hands, the curled gray nails covered with blood. He was still screaming in pain. The small zombie just lay there trying to catch his breath. His neck hurt so badly that he wanted to get up and run, but he had no strength left.

The big one now reacted strangely: He dropped to the floor next to the little guy, lifted him up into a sitting position, and said, almost nicely, "Can you look at my head? It's stinging and throbbing!"

The small zombie was surprised by the change of tone in his adversary's voice. He gently pulled the tangled bloody hair apart, and said in a raspy voice, "You have a bigggg scratch. It looks like somebody has finally punished you for always wanting to kill me." He chuckled.

Not waiting for a response, he ripped a piece off his torn shirt, gently wiped the blood off the big guy's skull, and then placed pressure on the wound until the blood stopped.

"I think you'll be all right now. Do you still want to fight with me?" The big zombie looked at the small one with his blood-shot eyes, and gave him a crooked smirk, which was meant to be a smile.

"No, I want to say thank you for taking care of me. I'm so sorry for having a bad temper; I know I almost strangled you." He extended his hand to the small zombie. "Let's be friends again."

The small zombie was no fool and revealing his toothless grin he said, "Are you kidding? I don't trust you. You've done this to me many times. You were violent when you were alive, and you're worse now, you ghostly beast. I have a feeling you'll come after me even now and then drag me here again next year like you do every year."

In the blink of an eye the small zombie's body changed into a small white cloud and he vanished.

"OMG they *are* ghosts!" Antonio whirred loudly, laughing like crazy.

"What is that horrible sound?" The big zombie screamed. "Whatever it is, I can't stand it." He looked around but didn't see anything. Annoyed, he too turned into a small cloud like the other zombie, and dispersed into the air.

Antonio didn't know whether to scream or be delighted at what he'd just experienced. "I can't believe what I've seen tonight!" It took him quite a while to come back to reality. He shook his head in disbelief and, mind cleared, took up his journey again. This time he could see the glistening ocean shimmer in the far distance and headed in that direction.

Chapter eighteen

Rachel's dad talked to the Molinos every day to encourage them to be positive about Antonio. "I expect to see him here any day now," he kept repeating. However, his cheerfulness and positive attitude no longer had the power to convince Rachel. She cried often and had a hard time concentrating on her studies. She tried her best but each day became harder than the day before.

Alexander was behaving like the best brother ever. Every day after school he came to Rachel's room and they did their homework together. After they finished, they sat down on the floor and played with their new and freshly shaved puppy, who they had named Pucci, and their little cat Cookie. They were amused at how well Pucci and Cookie got along.

Rachel put on the TV. At first Pucci curled his tail between his legs and scurried away. Cookie spread himself on the floor in a dignified manner and calmly watched the screen. Pucci then peeked from the corner of the room, and when he determined it was safe, cautiously walked over and lay down next to Cookie. Their antics made Rachel and Alexander laugh, and helped Rachel with her anxiety over Antonio's whereabouts.

Seeing that his sister had relaxed a little bit, Alexander took advantage of the moment to say some encouraging words to her. "How I wish I were with Antonio all this time and I could share in his adventures! Can you imagine the animals and birds he's had a chance to see? Believe me, Sis, he's out there having fun, seeing a whole different world, and yet you're here worried about him! It's all for nothing. Knowing Antonio, I'm sure he knows exactly what he's doing."

Alexander turned a few cartwheels across the room, managing not to destroy anything in the process. Then he made clownish faces at Rachel and tried to cheer her up again. "Calm down and stop this crying; you'll scare Pucci and Cookie. Look, he'll be here before we know it. Why don't you come for a bicycle ride with me and my friend, Don?" He wouldn't stop until she finally laughed and fetched her bicycle helmet.

Chapter nineteen

Antonio truly had a bird's eye view of the land ahead. Even in an airplane he would've been unable to observe the beauty of his surroundings as well as he could now. The mountains, illuminated by the bright city lights, acted as a protective ring around the town. The city itself was snaked with multiple roads of blinking lights.

He wanted to find out the name of the city and was anxious to land there. However, for some reason his wings kept moving forward at high speeds and he had no control over them. At this point in his journey he knew better than to question the powers that controlled his movements, so he just went with it.

Suddenly his antennas started to pull him over to a more sparsely lit area: He knew this was the sign to land. Passing very low above the city his wings became more flexible, and he gradually drifted down without any effort.

Ahead, a series of small homes covered in bright red roofs beckoned, surrounded by colorful gardens full of flowers, green bushes and tall trees. Wings fluttering, he hovered over the area until he felt safe: The homes ahead actually looked very inviting. It was late and the lights were on at all the entrances; every once in while the quiet was punctuated by the excited bark of a dog. Antonio felt right at home.

He was drawn to land at a particular home. A large brick patio lay surrounded by trees, with a shimmering fountain in the middle illuminated by a single pink light. He perched on the concrete edge of the fountain and admired the small sculpture of an angel in the center. How her face reminded him of Rachel! Maybe this was a sign of some sort. He wished that this were Rachel's home, but instinctively he knew it wasn't.

"Although I'm *almost* at Rachel's home," he thought. "Oh, please, let me be human again!" Antonio glanced at his reflection in the water and saw no change. He was reminded of how far he had come and yet how far he still had to go. Antonio sighed and wondered if he'd ever be transformed into human shape again.

He was thirsty. His practical side took over and he decided to go for a drink. Bending slightly, he sipped a bit of the crystal-clear cold water. He noticed little gold fish in the water, happily frolicking from one end of the pond to the other. Antonio took some deep calming breaths. As he sipped again he was surprised to hear the strange yet comforting laugh that had followed him on his journey and this time a gentle fragrance of gardenias also perfumed the air. He suddenly realized that the magic presence that was protecting him was a feminine one. "Wow! Now I know she's still with me, but who is she?" He smiled, and his large eyes sparkled in the reflection of the pool below.

Then Antonio lifted his head and looked around just in case this time his protector would show herself, but there was no one. Only the leaves on the peach tree rustled, something gentle stirred the air, and then it became still and silent.

His thirst gone and feeling tired, Antonio nestled under the peach tree in between its green leaves, wrapped his wings close to his body and fell asleep.

Chapter twenty

When Antonio opened his eyes it was still dark. He felt something crawling all over his body and he *hated* crawling things! He jumped up. In the flickering light of the fountain he saw a small army of black ants, falling off his body and scurrying in every direction.

He left that place in a hurry and scampered over to the edge of the fountain where he took a few sips of water and sat thinking of his next step. His head began to hurt and his antennas hung limply, looking like wilted miniature clover buds. The sign that it was time to eat! Immediately he sat next to a lush pink peach, and as he dipped his mouth in its sweetness, his eyes wandered.

Surprise hit Antonio right between his beady ruby eyes. On a small branch almost hidden by thick green leaves, Red was also dipping his beak in a peach! Then Red jumped on the branch across from him and began to chirp softly. Although he wondered what his *amigo* was doing here, Antonio was really glad to see Red again. It sure felt good to have a friend on this journey! They exchanged welcoming glances as they picked on the fruit, not paying attention to the sunrise and the other birds around them.

The house was still asleep. Antonio eagerly waited to see if someone would open a door or window: He still didn't know what city or town he was in and he was looking for clues. He noticed that Red was napping, so he decided to fly around and check for hints to his whereabouts. He flew just above the house and made a few rounds, but there was nothing to give him any clues. "Oh, well! I guess I'll find out sooner or later."

He returned to the fountain, drank more water, and soon fluttered over to a pink hibiscus bush next to the window. To his disappointment, the shades were still drawn and he couldn't see a thing. Antonio decided to perch on a geranium plant hanging from the window and wait until someone opened the shades.

Suddenly he felt something grabbing and squashing him! He tried to wiggle away but it was useless. He was trapped in a boy's hand and the more Antonio tried to squirm away the more he was squeezed. The boy said, "This is the most unusual bird I've ever seen." He shouted: "Hey, David, come over here; I have something to show you!"

"Hold on Rob, let me get my books and I'll be right there." In no time David emerged, skipping from the side door. He laughed at seeing Rob tightly holding Antonio in his hand.

"Terrific! It'll be great to take him to school," David exclaimed. "This is really the strangest locust I've ever seen."

Rob sounded annoyed. "He is *not* a locust; to me he looks like a bird."

David argued, "He's a locust," and then glanced at his watch. "We have to hurry or we'll be late for school." Rob ran into the house and emerged with his book bag hanging on his shoulder and a shoebox holding Antonio. Both boys ran through gardens and sidewalks to school.

Antonio was darting back and forth in the box, sick from fright and frustration. "How could I be so stupid to be caught like this? I made it through the desert, got really sick and even escaped from zombies, and now when I'm close to finding Rachel, I let myself be captured! What will they do to me? And where is Red?" He finally stopped scurrying and lay down on the bottom of the box to make plans for his escape.

Chapter twenty-one

David and Rob were identical twins about Antonio's age and height, physically fit and slender. They were dressed in navy blue trousers and white shirts, with identical Justin Bieber haircuts.

They ran all the way to school so when they entered the classroom they were short of breath. All the other students were already at their desks, looking at them and the white shoebox curiously. David and Rob couldn't wait to tell them about the surprise sitting in the box.

It was too late to give the other kids the scoop since their smiling, stylish, and highly efficient teacher, Mrs. Cole, had just walked in. "Good morning class," she began. Then she noticed the shoebox on Rob's desk.

Curiously, she lifted her dark eyebrows as she walked briskly over to him. She asked, "Rob, what are you hiding in there? May I see it?" Rob excitedly lifted the lid but gasped when he looked inside. He covered his mouth with his hand: On the bottom of the box, Antonio lay on his back only lightly moving his legs, suffocating from lack of air.

Rob, not waiting to answer Mrs. Cole, grabbed the locust and ran to the bathroom. He turned on the water spigot and let drops of cool water drip into Antonio's mouth.

In the meantime, David explained to his classmates and the teacher about this most unusual catch they had found. Their teacher, calm as always, just asked the class to start their computers, and the lesson began.

Outside, Antonio came back to life after filling his tiny lungs with air. Chirping loudly, he noticed that the slight fragrance of gardenias filled the air. That gave Antonio even more strength.

Rob, feeling Antonio trying to wiggle out of his hand, wrapped his fingers even tighter around him and ran back to the classroom anxious to show his find to the class. With one quick look at Antonio, the teacher said, "This is definitely a locust. Compared to others he is very large and the whiskers on his head are so unique that we'll have to take him to the Natural Science Museum for identification and study: I'm sure it will be a most unusual addition to our Irvine Museum."

Antonio trembled with excitement at hearing the name of the city. "I'm in Irvine. Laguna Beach isn't far from here! I've practically arrived at my goal and yet I'm trapped!" Antonio chirped and twittered loudly. So loud in fact, that his locust sounds were unbearable to the students.

Boys and girls rushed to cover their ears. Antonio screamed again. "Take him out, let him go, we can't listen to him anymore!" the kids complained. Antonio screamed even louder.

"Okay, okay. I'm taking him out." However, instead of letting Antonio free, Rob left him in the box, covered him with the lid left slightly open for air circulation, and kept the box on his desk.

Antonio wouldn't stop his loud tweets and chirps. The class was so annoyed that Mrs. Cole finally walked over to Rob and said, "Rob, take him into the hallway; after school we'll bring him to the museum." Rob grabbed the box and placed it on the hallway floor right outside the class-room door.

Antonio became alive with hope. "Now I've got a real chance to escape!" He knew somehow that he had to lift that lid. He looked up; he could see a sliver of light between the lid and the box. He fluttered his wings with all his strength, pushed the lid with his hooked claws and lifted it, sliding it to the side. "I'm free!" This time there were screams of joy when he saw the hallway door open to the outside.

Once out of reach he flew straight up into the air with excitement. "Goodbye silly boys! I'm free! Soon I'll see Rachel and tomorrow we'll celebrate our birthdays together. Nothing can stop me now!" Yet as he flew away his breathing became shallow; he was at a high altitude and he'd forgotten that he hadn't had anything to eat since he'd been captured.

He flew over the top of the nearest mountain searching for a place to land. In spite of his hunger he was amazed at the sheer beauty of the Pacific Ocean beside him: The reflection of the clear blue sky created a mirrored surface, so smooth it appeared one could walk on it.

Just below him he spotted the red and white roofs of large homes, all wrapped in gardens bursting with colorful flowers. "I need to stop in one of the gardens and find a fruit tree; I'm starving." He glanced once again at the mountains. In the glare of the morning sun, they appeared swathed in transparent white veils that sloped down to the valleys, creating contrasting lines against the dark of the mountains that curved in the shape of crescents.

He thought he was witnessing paradise. "Rachel is so lucky to live here with her family. I hope my parents will come here too and we will be one happy family again." He swallowed hard.

Gradually he let his wings slow down and flew forward, searching for a place to land. His antennas pulled him sharply to the right and he glanced ahead. Many boats floated on the sparkling water along wooden docks. "Wow! This must be the Newport Beach Marina that Rachel talked about, where she often walks with her parents and Alexander." His eyes wandered over the countless big and small yachts swaying on the blue-green ocean.

Antonio then flew into the garden of a nearby one-story home surrounded by a low white fence covered in hibiscus and bursting with rose bushes of all colors. He sat down on a fully opened pink rose and enjoyed the sweet pollen mixed with morning dew. As he ate, he watched the sun shimmer against a horizon scattered with white fluffy clouds. Antonio felt so elated about his dangerous trip almost coming to an end, that he completely forgot all his worries and just enjoyed the moment.

Chapter twenty-two

Thanks to Alexander's clownish antics, Rachel was managing to keep up her spirits. Both kids were lounging in her room, playing with Pucci and Cookie. Alexander looked up from petting Cookie. "Just imagine how lucky you are to have a birthday on the same day as your best friend," he said. "And not only that, but you've also been able to celebrate together for thirteen years: I wish I had a friend like that!" He quickly added, "I'm so sure that Antonio will be here on time for both of your birthdays that you should go ahead and invite everyone and plan the celebration. We need to have some fun!"

He threw his arm around her shoulder. "He'll be here even if he has to fly like *her*!" Alexander laughingly pointed to his sister's pink pajamas with the figure of Spider Woman. He jumped up, spread his arms like wings and ran around the room jumping from furniture to furniture. "Zoom, zoom! I'm here Rachel," he sang in an imitation of Antonio. Pucci barked and chased him; Cookie decided on a more a dignified stance and sat away from the mayhem.

He was so funny and Rachel was laughing so loudly that their mom, Juliette, ran up the stairs to see what they were up to. When she opened the door to Rachel's bedroom, Alexander was laying on the floor, arms akimbo, hair gone wild and still making funny faces amid the laughter. She was so thankful for her son's positive energy! Of course, Juliette knew Alexander was the added sparkle in the family: He made everybody laugh and always maintained an optimistic outlook on life.

Rachel jumped over the prone Alexander, ran to her mother and embraced her. "Mommy, Alexander's convinced me: I want to have my birthday party after all. I'll call my friends to come to the party tomorrow. Will you help me plan everything?"

Juliette was very happy to see Rachel so lively again. "I absolutely will do that, darling. And to make it even more appealing you can tell them you'll have a disc jockey. I will make the arrangements and you can dance on the terrace in the garden. We will make it very beautiful; tell all your friends to be here at six o'clock."

For once Alexander was quiet, sitting on the floor and feeling very proud as he gazed up at his mom and Rachel. The two were hugging each other, talking about the party and not paying any attention to him. His plan had worked: He slipped out of the room on his tiptoes. "I'm so glad to see a happy home again." His impish smile revealed a cute small gap between his upper teeth.

Feeling like he'd completed a job well done, Alexander pulled up his navy blue baggy sweatpants and straightened his tee shirt with the large Superman figure on the chest. He felt a little like Superman himself! Now it was up to Antonio. "Come on Antonio, I'm counting on you," he said softly. He raked long fingers through his short blond hair and ran to the back door, rushing to soccer practice.

Chapter twenty-three

Antonio opened his eyes to glimpse traces of a gentle sunset spreading across the sky; he hadn't even realized he'd fallen asleep. He glanced over at the adjoining marina, then down at the small shimmering fountain. His heart beat with excitement as his thoughts turned once again to journey's end. He was going to see Rachel soon and it didn't matter anymore if he was either boy or locust: He trusted his fate. As if in agreement, a soft laugh echoed for a split second and dispersed in the gardenia fragranced air.

He was getting ready to fly when suddenly he noticed a small bird over by the rose bush. The bird looked like he was in some sort of pain. Antonio took a closer look: It was Red! His friend was barely clinging to the branch, his little limp body resting flat and belly down, his wings drooping.

In a split second Antonio fluttered over to Red. First Antonio touched Red with one clawed foot to try to stir him awake. When that didn't work he tried to lift Red with his hooked arms, but the bird was too heavy for him to carry. Frustrated, Antonio began to jiggle him with both arms; finally Red opened his eyes.

Now Antonio had to figure out how to get Red over to the fountain for some water. He fluttered to the branch just an inch under the bird and moved his wings up and down brushing the bird's belly. Ouch! Antonio felt the bird drop to his own tiny back. Carrying his heavy burden and moving his wings rapidly, Antonio landed just on the edge of the fountain. Gently he let Red slip off his back and onto the fountain's shelf where he urged drops of water to fall on Red's beak. Antonio watched until he saw his friend move his head and noted that he was swallowing drops of water. What a relief! Antonio's next task was to find some food.

He looked up and spotted a nearby raspberry bush flush with red berries. Carefully he fetched one raspberry with his mouth, flew down, placed it next to the bird's beak and flew back to get more fruit. Upon his return the fruit was gone and the bird's wings were resting closer to his body. Antonio did this many times until Red had his fill.

Finally it was Antonio's turn to eat. He sat down, dipped his mouth in the fruit and ate greedily, hungry from his heavy labors. Once he'd finished eating, Antonio looked at his friend: Red seemed to have regained his strength.

The odd couple sat and looked at each other intensely. Then Red let out a loud chirp, moved his wings and surprisingly, nestled right next to Antonio, brushing his wing against Antonio's leg. This closeness wouldn't last long.

The window above opened and startled them. They flew up and soared together above the red roofs and gardens. Antonio's antennas took over navigation and began pulling him towards a large playground filled with noisy children. Red was not far behind.

Suddenly his antennas gave a strong pull towards a sprawling building surrounded by a sizeable fenced area. The pair zoomed in on the building's sign, which read "Plaza Vista School", the name of Rachel's school! Antonio couldn't believe how close he was to his goal. The familiar perfume surrounded them both and a soft laugh vibrated in the air. Antonio's heart was filled with equal parts of hope and longing.

Chapter twenty-four

It was Saturday, May twelve. Rachel's home and its garden were decorated with colorful ribbons and balloons. Cords of bright butterfly lights were strung throughout the party area. Four long tables were covered in tablecloths decorated with butterflies and ladybugs; matching plates and napkins were in place.

Rachel and her mom were in the kitchen putting the last touches on the food: Finger sandwiches, macaroni salad, chicken nuggets and green salads mixed with different fruits and nuts. "Mommy, you are so clever," Rachel said. "My friends will never guess that you serve only healthy food! They'll devour everything, it looks so good!" They both laughed and hugged. "You make my birthday party so special every year," Rachel continued. "You spoil me."

On the surface everything was great and Rachel really tried to be happy, but her private thoughts were much different. How she wished that Antonio were here! She knew his personality well and realized that he would love the party and have a great time with all her new friends. A few tears dared to come to her eyes and she brushed them away quickly. She was determined to put on a good face for her family.

"Soon the DJ will arrive and then the guests. I hope grandma won't be stuck in traffic again; I always worry about her driving in the city."

"Don't worry," Juliette replied. "She is a good driver and I'm sure she will be here any minute: We're so fortunate to have her so close to us."

Rachel forced a bright smile on her pretty face. She asked her mom, "Should I wear the long pink strapless dress with the butterflies on it?"

"Yes, absolutely," replied Juliette. "You look so pretty in it and it will match the decorations in the garden! I had totally forgotten about that dress."

Before going up to her room to change, Rachel once more gazed at the decorated patio. She sighed: With its flickering lights and beautiful colors it looked like a magical royal garden from a fairy tale. She knew it sounded childish, but she thought the only missing detail was the prince!

Just at that moment her dad came home. "Wow, Rachel, I'm not sure if I'm in the right place: It's so beautiful and so are you!" he said playfully. "How are you, my princess?" Barely blinking back tears Rachel ran into his embrace, kissed his cheek and aimed for the kitchen door. "Daddy, I'm late; I'll see you later."

As she climbed the stairs Rachel finally let out her pent up feelings, flung herself on the bed next to her cat and cried. Cookie was startled out of his daily nap but instinctively knew something was wrong with his mistress. So Cookie gently nudged Rachel with his little black nose and kissed her face all over. Charmed, Rachel stopped crying and stood up.

"Do you think Antonio will come to my party?" she asked her kitty.

"Meow," Cookie answered as he wrapped himself around Rachel's legs. "I'm glad I asked for your opinion," Rachel replied amused, as she opened the door to let Cookie out.

Rachel wiped her tears and splashed cold water on her face. She slipped on the pink dress and quickly pulled her long hair into a ponytail with a lacy pink band. She added a touch of lip-gloss and slid flat sparkling pink sandals on her feet. Finally she looked in the mirror: She flashed a smile and felt ready to face the world.

Chapter twenty-five

Rachel ran down directly to the garden and immediately saw her grandma. "Grandma Bobbi, I'm so glad to see you!" Bobbi had just arrived and was hugging Juliette: She was holding a small pink package in one hand. Waving the other hand at Rachel, she said a warm hello and they rushed into each other's arms to embrace tightly. Bobbi said, "Rachel, do you remember when I came to visit you in Mexico for the first time? You were four years old."

"You took my hand and pulled me to the patio to show me a plant on a table. Between the leaves of a geranium plant you had placed a big green plastic locust that seemed to stare at me with his round ruby eyes."

"Yes, Grandma I remember it well: I was so happy to see you."

Bobbi handed her a pink package. "Well, this is a book I've written just for you, all about that locust. *You* gave me the inspiration to write it!" Rachel grabbed the book and held it close to her heart, exclaiming, "Grandma, you wrote a book for *me*? I love you so much and I can't wait to read it! Grandma, you look so beautiful." They hugged once more.

"You're the beautiful one, my baby, and you are growing more beautiful every day even as I get older." Bobbi took a deep breath and stepped back to look at her granddaughter. "I can't believe you look just like your mom when she was thirteen. Where did the time go?"

"Okay you two, that's enough; you're making me cry!" said Juliette with pride and a few tears in her voice. "You *both* grow more beautiful every day. Take a look at yourself, Mom: You look really great; why, you could be my sister!"

Bobbi indeed looked very young. Her dark hair was pulled into a perfect bun on top of her head, completely revealing her yet unlined face. She radiated health and energy with her glowing skin and bright white smile. Her high-heels accentuated a slender frame and gave her the appearance of being taller than she really was. Bobbi attributed her youthful looks to her healthy diet and daily workouts and made sure her family took care of themselves as well.

Rachel's father was watching them from the side with a melancholy look on his face. "Three generations of beautiful ladies, how lucky we are and how proud I am of them. I only wish *my* Mom were here as well."

Only Alexander was missing from this family portrait since he was still at soccer practice and was expected to be home any minute. The DJ arrived through the back gate and all of them went to help with his equipment. Roberto lent him a hand setting up under a flowering pink bougainvillea bush that trailed up a wooden trellis. All the multihued lights were on, waiting for the guests to arrive.

At a quarter to six, Alexander sprinted through the back garden, hugged his grandma and dashed upstairs to take a shower. In just a few minutes he walked back downstairs wearing his baggy jeans and American eagle tee shirt. His hair was spiked with so much gel that Rachel couldn't help but laugh. "You look like a porcupine," she said happily. Her brother grinned as the whole family laughed.

Rachel had invited her entire class of eighteen to attend the party and they soon began to arrive by twos and threes. They were a great looking group of young "fashionistas", wearing all of the latest fashion trends. Some of the girls wore long or short colorful strapless dresses, others had on very short skirts with off-shoulder tops. Their shoes sparkled like tiny stars in various hues. The boys looked equally dapper in their bright polo shirts and khaki pants, most with various versions of the spiked hair look that was so popular.

Rachel walked over to her grandma and whispered in her ear. "Look at how beautiful and fun my friends are; I wish so much that Antonio could be here like every other year!"

Bobbi held her close and whispered back. "Go and enjoy your time with your friends and keep him close in your heart. He will be here soon; positive thinking is very important." She gave Rachel a gentle push.

"Thanks, Grandma." Rachel ran off to dance. The DJ spun the Justin Bieber hit "Baby, Baby" and everyone was up dancing, clapping and singing along.

"What a happy, joyful scene to watch teens having a wonderful time!" She took a deep breath. "How I wish I had my life ahead of me again: I miss my youthful years. Where did the time go?" Her eyes became misty.

She felt like her heart was caught in her throat as she gazed at the starry sky and thought of her husband being some place among them. "Twinkle once and let me know which star you are," she whispered. "I miss you so much, you know. How I wish you were here with our grandchildren and me. You would love them as much as I do, and you would be so proud of them." Tears welled in her eyes. She turned her attention back to the children and started to smile again.

Chapter twenty-six

Antonio happily toured around the school accompanied by his now faithful sidekick, Red. Knowing that this was Rachel's school, he couldn't get enough of the view. All of a sudden he noticed a group of boys at soccer practice in the wide field ahead. He was so jealous! He and Red zoomed in for a closer look and couldn't believe what they saw: It was Alexander, Rachel's brother, playing soccer in the field below! Wait a minute; did Red recognize Alexander, too? How could that be?

Antonio didn't have time to figure out this new mystery. The boys below had stopped playing and each was going his separate way. They had to follow Alexander! "Here's my chance to find Rachel's home at last!" twittered Antonio with excitement. Red chirped loudly in response.

It was easy to follow Alexander who was now singing brashly and cheerfully as he sprinted home, obviously in a big hurry. For a brief moment Antonio felt the slight tug of his antennas and then all was still. He thought of his magical and yet unknown helper. "Thank you for helping me reach here safely," he said. "I guess you realize I can find the rest of the way on my own now."

The sun was flirting with the ocean to the west; in a few minutes darkness would embrace the evening and, if he didn't hurry, it would be too late to see Rachel on her birthday. It almost didn't matter that he was still an ugly locust and that he didn't know what would become of him: He had come home to Rachel. He whispered to her very softly, "I'm here, Rachel. I came to you, just like I promised."

Immediately to the left colorful lights beamed brightly from a nearby garden and he could see Alexander running through the gate. He flew in closer to check it out in detail. Reaching the tallest tree in the garden, he settled between the branches and witnessed a charming site. In front lay a garden beautifully decorated and laid out for a party, with pretty tables laden with food. A DJ had set up under a colorful bush to spin his music and guests dressed in colorful clothes were arriving in happy clusters. The scene was picture perfect: But where was Rachel? His heart beating fast and his friend Red by his side, Antonio once more settled in to wait.

Soon there was much music and laughter, dancing and eating. The DJ played all the top hits by Justin Bieber, Mariah Carey and Taylor Swift. The guests looked like they were having a great time. "I can't believe I'm here." Tears stung Antonio's eyes and a very soft sound came out of his throat. "I'm here Rachel." Then he saw her, dancing with her brother Alexander: Antonio couldn't hold his emotions any longer so he cried out piercingly, "Rachel I'm here! I want to dance with you; I want to be with your friends!" Unfortunately he was still a locust and the cries echoed so loudly that he interrupted the party.

Suddenly the music stopped and all heads were turned towards the trees and bushes on the far side of the garden. "What *was* that strange sound?" everyone asked. No one talked as they all paused to try to hear the sound again, but it didn't come back. The DJ put on Taylor Swift's "The Story of Us" and soon everybody was dancing, laughing, talking and clapping hands.

Rachel's mom humorously dismissed the kids' reaction to the strange sound. "It has to be some exotic bird that doesn't like today's loud music!" she laughed, as she spoke to Bobby. "After all, many birds make funny noises before they go to sleep."

However, Bobby had an odd feeling. She was curious about the strange noises coming from the trees, decided to get some bread and crumbled cookies to place on the benches near the trees to attract the birds. She disappeared between the bushes to do so. Looking up and around, Bobby didn't notice anything unusual, so she left the food on the benches and walked back to join Juliette and Roberto in the kitchen.

Antonio saw everything and almost gave up hope to attend the party as his human self. He flew down to the bench and cried out softly.

"I really need your help, my magical friend. I realize that I had to pay for disobeying my parents, but I am so close now. Please turn me back into a human! I want to be a normal guy again! I want to dance with Rachel and hug my parents. I promise that I've learned my lesson!"

Instantly Antonio smelled the special fragrance that had accompanied him on his journey, the strong perfume wafting through the air all around him. It all came back to him now! He remembered that his grandma used to smell like that all the time. He'd always loved that scent and hugging her close to smell it; the fragrance made him feel loved and safe. This time he whispered, "*Abuelita*, I realize now it was always *you*! You know how much I love you and miss you. I remember you used to tell me you'd always wanted to come to America so I know you understand. Thank you for protecting me by changing me into the locust. I love you Grandma: You're the best. Please change me back to your Antonio now. Please." He looked up at the starry sky knowing she was there, watching over him from heaven.

Antonio's body suddenly felt incredibly warm and he could hear himself speak! "OMG, I have my voice back!" But that wasn't all. Still sitting on the bench he looked down at himself and was amazed to see hands and feet, arms and legs and a normal body. And he was dressed in the clothes he wore when he set out on his journey! The fuzzy legs, the hands that looked like claws, the wings, antennas and even the mouth of the locust lay on the bench next to him.

"Thank you, *Abuelita*; I love you!" Antonio was overwhelmed. He glanced around, looking for Red. Across from him on another bench sat his best friend and soccer mate, Mario, grinning broadly! The red beak and multiple feathers that had belonged to Red were scattered around him. Antonio ran to Mario and gave him a big hug, "You are such a good friend; thanks for all your help!"

"I have no idea what happened here," Mario said sheepishly. "When I heard you were gone I ran away from home and the next thing I knew I was with you on your adventures. And what adventures; I'm exhausted!" His eyes were closing swiftly and in a split second he was asleep, stretched out on the bench. Antonio laughed. Typical, crazy Mario!

At the edge of the bench a small guitar rested; Alexander must have left it there. Antonio had an idea: He grabbed the guitar and began to play Rachel's favorite Mexican song by Raul de Blasio *"El Triste"*, singing softly in accompaniment. Just at that moment the DJ took a break and no loud music was playing.

The guests became silent when they heard the beautiful strings of a guitar coming from the other side of the garden. However, Rachel was anything but silent. "Antonio, Antonio, Antonio!" she cried. She ran through the garden towards the sounds of the gentle music. Her best girl-friends Bella and Stephanie followed her, leaving the crowd behind. Soon they were short of breath and they stopped and walked back to the group.

Antonio, now seeing Rachel, dropped the guitar on the bench and ran towards her as fast as he could. He hugged her tightly and whispered, "I love you Rachel. I've missed you so much!" Holding hands they smiled through their tears as they walked back to the party. Rachel happily shouted out to her friends, "Everybody, this is my best friend Antonio who came from Mexico just to be with me on my birthday!"

The DJ was a quick study and put on "Thank God I Found You" by Mariah Carey. All Rachel's friends held hands and made a circle around them, looking at each other and happy for their friend. When the song ended, the DJ began to sing "Happy Birthday" and all the kids joined in as the adults, who'd been in the kitchen getting everything ready for this moment, stepped out into the patio with the cake.

Juliette was carrying the delicious confection, which flickered with thirteen candles. She was flanked by both Bobbi and Roberto. Juliette quickly placed the cake on the table as they all stared at the tender scene in front of them.

Roberto pulled the iPhone from his pocket, pushed automatic dial and said to his friends in Mexico, "OMG! Antonio is here."

The End

About The Author

Barbara Juliette Klinger was born and educated in Poland where early on she discovered her love of the poetry and literature of Polish authors as well as those of international repute. After immigrating to the United States she dedicated her whole life to family, as companion to her physician husband and mother of their children. To maintain her creative spirit, in her spare time she wrote poetry and soon became recognized as a distinguished member of The International Society of Poets. Over the years she has been published in many anthologies including the featured first page of the collection, *Celebration of Poets: Showcase Edition*. Eventually she published her own book of poetry, the highly acclaimed *Lost in a Maze of Dreams*. Barbara is also an accomplished artist and provided the cover artwork for this book.

The Song of the Locust is her first novel for young adults, inspired by her own life experiences and relationships with her family, especially her granddaughter Rachel. True to form, Barbara is already at work on her next novel.

ANGEL

I believe in my guardian angel.
I believe he protects me every day and night
I ask him endlessly to be with me
I carry him always with me
Deep in my heart and in my soul.
I believe in my guardian angel.
He gives me inspiration
He is beautiful and smart
He guides me, he gives me hope
When I feel lost and desperate
He insists everything will be all right.

SHELL

We live inside a shell
We think the ocean will never spill us out
Suddenly a wave rises and spins us onto the sand
Suddenly our destiny is solely resting in our hands

Rachel and Antonio as drawn
by Rachel, the author's young granddaughter.

The author's grandchildren, Alexander and Rachel

"We should always cherish the voices of our children."
Barbara Juliette Klinger

4849862R00070

Printed in Great Britain
by Amazon.co.uk, Ltd.,
Marston Gate.